"Com[...]na," he murmured

"Why, Matt?" she asked. "You don't really need me. You are the most self-sufficient man I know. I know you hate failure—my leaving you has hurt your pride."

His hands clenched into fists, and then he pulled her toward him, pressing his mouth down on hers. She felt the thrusting power of his hips and went limp in his arms.

It was too late. He laughed triumphantly, and she shuddered, feeling the strong beat of her own blood pounding, drowning any resistance she might have felt....

"Please," she gasped. "Please . . . it's too late. It's over."

"You really believe it's over?" he asked hoarsely, "when I can make you want me like this!"

English born **Jennifer Williams** didn't start writing until her fifth child started school, when her husband bought her a typewriter and told her to stop talking about it and get on with it. When her husband became a lock keeper on the River Trent, they moved to a cottage on an island in the middle of the river—very pretty, very isolated. Her first book was a historical novel, but she prefers writing romances with their happy endings. When her husband retired, she took over his job, becoming the first woman lock keeper on the Trent. She finds both her careers interesting, but admits writing has the edge.

BROKEN DREAMS
Jennifer Williams

Harlequin Books

TORONTO • NEW YORK • LONDON
AMSTERDAM • PARIS • SYDNEY • HAMBURG
STOCKHOLM • ATHENS • TOKYO • MILAN

Original hardcover edition published in 1991
by Mills & Boon Limited

ISBN 0-373-17100-5

Harlequin Romance first edition December 1991

For Jimmy, with all my love

BROKEN DREAMS

CHAPTER ONE

THE party was well under way by the time they arrived, though Matt abandoned Anna almost as soon as they walked through the door.

'Darling, Mr Yamiko has to leave for the airport in half an hour and I must have a final word with him before he goes. You'll be OK for five minutes, won't you?'

Anna shrank from what seemed like a solid wall of heat and noise. 'I don't know any of these people, Matt,' she protested.

The familiar irritation clouded his dark grey eyes. 'For heaven's sake, Anna, Sarah's here. You know her. I've asked her to introduce you around. She'll look after you.'

He left her abruptly, not giving her time to tell him that the last person she wanted to see was his cousin Sarah. She watched him push his way through the crowd, receiving smiles and greetings with his usual air of self-assured charm. Damn him, she thought, wishing she hadn't come.

Lights glittered; crystal chandeliers reflected in huge Venetian mirrors, shining on oyster satin drapes and gilded furniture. The vast room was very hot despite the air-conditioning and, feeling suffocated, Anna edged towards the far end where glass doors leading to the terrace stood open to the night.

'Anna, darling, how are you?' called a high, feminine voice.

Anna turned, a smile ready on her lips as she faced the other woman. 'Hello, Sarah. I'm fine, thank you,' she replied politely.

As always Matt's cousin was exquisitely dressed, this time in a dramatic sheath of white satin which was a perfect foil for her long dark hair, with diamonds shining at her ears and wrists. In her own plain yellow silk Anna felt colourless by comparison.

Sarah's grey eyes flicked over her knowingly, already dismissing her as a rival. 'I love the gown, though with your blonde hair I'd have thought yellow just a little bit chancy.' She put her head on one side as she looked Anna up and down. 'You've lost weight, haven't you? But then, I suppose one does in those circumstances ... and it seems to show more when one is fair-skinned, like you.' She smiled, cat-like, secure in her own dark beauty. 'We'll have to get Matt to spoil you a little, won't we? He's got some leave coming up. You can have my beach house in Malibu for a few weeks, if you like. Come to think of it, what if we made it a threesome? I'm sure Matt would love the idea.'

I'm sure he would too, Anna thought. Aloud she said, 'Perhaps you'd better ask him. We haven't finally decided where to spend his leave, though he did mention something about rock climbing in the Cairngorms.'

Casting about for an alternative, any alternative to the prospect of a cosy threesome in Sarah's Malibu beach house, Anna had said the first thing that came into her head, though she knew Sarah didn't believe her, and felt a fool when she replied, 'Rock climbing? Oh, dear, darling, I think we can do better than that, don't you?'

Anna's face ached from maintaining the false smile. She hated this woman so much, yet Matt would never forgive her if she made a scene here, at his uncle's yearly party for the senior executives of Barratt Oil.

She glanced around the room, searching restlessly for Matt's dark head. She couldn't see him and felt uneasy.

'Matt is still talking business with my father and the other execs,' said Sarah, sensing her anxiety. 'He asked me to look after you.' She took Anna's hand lightly in hers. 'Come along, the company wives are dying to meet you at long last. Don't you realise you're something of a celebrity, darling? The girl who actually managed to get Matthew Tennant to the altar. They're all so envious of you.' Her laughter tinkled like broken glass, though her pale grey eyes were cold and Anna wasn't fooled by her apparent friendliness; their hatred was mutual. It was bound to be, she supposed.

She didn't know why she had come here tonight. She had allowed Matt to persuade her despite the fact that she knew she would feel out of place among these people. The truth was she had run out of excuses. It was six months, after all ... She couldn't hide indefinitely, and, as people kept telling her, life must go on.

The wives all knew one another; Anna listened as they gossiped, clutching her wine glass, feeling like an outsider with her face pressed to the barrier separating her from them, a barrier which was partly of her own making. Though she knew also that they were bound to be wary of her. She was the wife of Matthew Tennant, the chairman's nephew, after all.

She saw curiosity in their eyes when they looked at her and wasn't surprised when, finally, one of them said, 'We were all so sorry to hear about...' The woman's voice trailed off into embarrassed silence and her eyes slid away from Anna's.

Sarah sighed heavily. 'For goodness' sake, Iris...'

Iris glanced apologetically at Anna. 'Oh...I'm sorry for mentioning it. I didn't mean to upset you.'

Anna saw her confusion and pitied her. 'That's all right,' she said and, throwing a sharp look in Sarah's direction, wondered what she had told them as the conversation returned to safer topics: clothes, hairdressers, food, and of course the company. It was as though none of them had an identity other than that of company wife, Anna thought, realising how comfortable it would be to be able to settle quietly into such a role herself. It was what Matt wanted of her, and once she had thought she could be content to go along with his wishes. But that was before, when love and marriage had been fresh and bright. Now, she knew better.

The talk suddenly drifted away into self-conscious silence as James Barratt himself approached the group, and Sarah went to slip her arm through his.

'Daddy, come and say hello to Anna. Matt's finally persuaded her to leave her shell.'

Anna cringed as she felt James's critical glance appraising her. He was a tall man, big, overpoweringly handsome in middle age. James could be very charming, if one ignored his ruthless reputation, and the coldness in his pale grey eyes.

'Good to see you among us again, Anna,' he said, his tone suggesting it was about time. He took her arm and led her a little way away from the group of wives. 'You're looking much better than when I saw you last.'

'Thank you,' she replied, unable to think of anything else to say. The last occasion they had met had been just after she came out of hospital. He had called to bring flowers and stayed precisely five minutes.

'Hmm . . . as I told Matthew at the time, the best thing for you would be to forget that unfortunate episode and start again. You're both young, there's no reason why you shouldn't have other, healthy children.'

It was like telling someone who had just lost a beloved pet dog to go out and buy a puppy, Anna thought, not trusting herself to reply, seeing Sarah's malicious smile out of the corner of her eye.

'As you know,' James continued, 'I like to think of Barratt's as a family company. We project a wholesome image that appeals to the man in the street. He knows he can trust us and our products, and I like the people who work for me to be family men. Families mean togetherness, and children.' He eyed her from beneath thick dark brows. 'Children are our future, Anna. You get my drift?'

She smiled weakly, having heard all this before. James Barratt saw himself as a kind of corporation patriarch, which was all very well until he started interfering in the private lives of those who worked for him. 'It's not as easy as that, Mr Barratt,' she remarked coolly.

'Rubbish! Having children is a simple matter of biology. Think positive, Anna!' he said bracingly, patting her arm. 'I've already had a word with Matthew; the rest is up to you.' And with that final shot he left her.

The wives were discussing a new French restaurant and, with a feeling of relief, Anna was able to slip away from the group unnoticed. She made for the terrace doors and stepped outside into the hot dark night.

The terrace was spacious and private, with wrought-iron furniture and green plants in terracotta urns. Below, the lights of Manhattan glittered and shone like a million fireflies, and Anna leaned against a vine-covered pillar, grateful that no one else had chosen to take refuge out here. It felt good to be alone, even for just a few moments.

Matt had insisted she come with him tonight. Another step forward, he had called it. The first had been accompanying him to New York for the Barratt Oil conference. She hadn't wanted to come. She had wanted to stay in London in her safe little mews cottage, where she didn't have to see anyone, or be forced to speak or think or feel.

She closed her eyes, resting her head against the pillar. Her face felt hot and she pushed damp tendrils of pale blonde hair back from her forehead. The air was still and humid and night insects threw themselves against the glass doors, eager to get to the light beyond. A moth settled on the yellow silk of her skirt and stayed a second before fluttering away to batter hopelessly against the glass. Anna felt like the moth, eager to leave a dark empty place and recapture the light and joy that had once been hers.

She heard voices, and the soft tinkle of feminine laughter as two people stepped on to the terrace. She pressed herself behind the pillar, not wanting to be discovered, and have to speak, and have them wondering why she was hiding out here alone in the dark.

Too late she recognised Sarah's voice, her laughter.

Sarah, with Matt, his voice low, soft-toned, amused. They walked to the balustrade without seeing Anna; Matt, tall and dark in his black suit, Sarah, slender and lovely in the white satin that hugged her figure like a second skin, her hair hanging loose to her waist in a shining cloak.

Hurting, aching, Anna watched as they whispered and laughed together. Sarah arched her body, curving into him, pressing herself against him, touching, stroking his cheek, her long red fingernails like drops of blood against his tanned skin.

His hands resting at her waist, sliding across the white satin to hold her as his head moved down to meet her waiting mouth . . .

Anna watched and felt pain clutch her, sharp, agonising, taking her breath. Then the blessed numbness closed in on her and she welcomed it like an old friend, going forward to meet it as it brought her the gift of oblivion.

She came to lying on a bed with a slippery pink satin spread. There was a light covered by a pink frilled shade by the bed, and, looking beyond it, Anna saw Matt sitting in a chair near by. He had taken off his jacket and bow-tie, and was watching her, nursing a whisky glass between his hands, hands that had touched and caressed Sarah's body... Anna shuddered, feeling sick to her soul.

He rose to his feet and came to look down at her, his face expressionless as he said, 'Are you feeling better?'

Anna nodded, not meeting his eyes. She swallowed; her mouth felt dry, her tongue swollen like a piece of sponge. She squeezed her eyes shut, trying to blot out the mind-pictures of Matt kissing Sarah Barratt.

'Do you think you can walk?' he asked, turning to pick up his jacket from the back of the chair.

She nodded again and swung her legs off the bed. He reached out to help her to her feet and she shook off his hand, unable to bear his touch.

She picked up her bag and moved to the dressing-table and, finding a comb, dragged it through her short blonde curls, staring at herself critically in the mirror.

She was pale, too pale, her mouth soft and vulnerable-looking, her blue eyes wide and shadowed. Compared with Sarah she was colourless, insignificant. She smeared on lipstick and blusher and, realising she was making a caricature of herself, wiped most of it off again.

'Are you ready?' Matt asked, his voice impatient, and she closed the bag immediately, despising herself. He slipped his jacket on and came to take her arm as they walked to the door.

Sarah came over to them, smiling maliciously. 'You really should take more water with it, darling,' she said, laughing as Anna stumbled.

'Save it!' Matt snapped, and Sarah pouted angrily.

'You're not going already?' she cried as they made for the door.

'Anna's had enough,' Matt replied shortly. 'Make our excuses, will you, Sarah? I have to get her back to the apartment.'

As if she were a parcel or something, Anna thought with resentment, pulling away from his arm.

'Of course. Poor Anna,' sighed Sarah, adding softly, 'and poor Matt.'

They were using a company apartment several floors down from the penthouse where the party was being held. Matt almost pushed her into the lift and she retreated to the far wall, putting as much distance as possible between them in the claustrophobic little space.

They passed the short journey in silence and, although she didn't meet his eyes once, she knew he was looking at her, knew also that if she glanced up she would see the familiar irritation in his expression.

Inside the apartment Anna went straight to her room without speaking to him. In her head rage simmered, and she yelled and screamed, hating him, hating Sarah, hating herself and the wretched weakness that refused to let the words be said out loud.

Why did she cling so obstinately to the moribund corpse of her marriage? Why could she not have the courage to let go?

She unzipped her dress and let it fall to the floor, then sat at the mirror to clean the make-up from her face, leaving it naked and smooth, exposed; deep blue eyes, high cheekbones with shadowed hollows beneath, a wide mouth, round chin. Her neck was slender and she wore a narrow gold chain with a tiny oval locket Matt had given her after they made love for the first time.

She smiled softly, remembering. How they had loved then. It had seemed as if all the love in the world had been hers, making her strong, invincible.

The door opened and Matt came into her room wearing just a towel round his hips. His chest muscles gleamed in the soft light from her bedside lamp, his dark hair was damp from the shower and his feet were bare.

Anna was suddenly breathless, waiting, nerves throbbing restlessly as she looked at him through the mirror. He stood behind her, hands hanging loosely by his sides. Their eyes met in the mirror and she turned away, afraid of the tension between them, afraid of the feelings that stirred inside her at the sight of his near-naked male beauty.

'Did you want something?' she asked, reaching for a robe to cover herself.

'Yes,' he murmured hoarsely. 'I want you.' His hand grasped her wrist and he drew her up to face him. He smelled fresh, of lemon soap and musky aftershave, and she closed her eyes against the hot rush of desire that rocked through her at his nearness.

He pulled her closer, his hands sliding around her, his mouth touching her neck, her throat, her shoulder. 'You've shut me out long enough, Anna, and I'm not prepared to wait any longer.'

'No, Matt, please.' She struggled feebly but he was so much stronger than she and her hands fluttered helplessly as she tried to keep her anger alive, to remember that only a short time ago he had held Sarah in his arms, touched Sarah, kissed her...

Then her palms came to rest on his shoulders, touching, pressing, loving the familiar smooth feel of his skin beneath her fingers. His arms tightened around her, crushing her against his body, moulding to breast, hip and thigh, his lips tasting hungrily as he lifted her and carried her to the bed.

She felt the cool softness of sheets against her skin, felt the hot weight of his body on hers, demanding, taking. They made love with silent urgency, his hands holding her, his breath mingling with her breath. The thunder of his heart, or was it hers?

The final crescendo, with soft, helpless cries and afterwards, weakness and lethargy, floating, misty vagueness. The sleep of exhaustion, held close, limbs entwined, bodies weightless, suspended in clouds.

They woke in the night and made love again. Anna held him, kissed him, listened as he whispered soft love-words, and responded to his practised caresses with a feeling close to despair.

Matthew lay awake, listening to Anna's soft breathing as she slept. Physically, their lovemaking had left his body relaxed, though he knew it had solved nothing between them.

He sighed and shifted slightly, feeling her move against him, and tightened his hold around her. Now, in the warm dark night, he could even pretend a kind of contentment, but he was very well aware that morning would bring the closed expression back to her eyes, shutting him out. Always shutting him out . . .

Matt was up first in the morning and Anna, waking alone in her bed, felt the heaviness of depression and self-loathing settle on her. Her body ached and she went through to shower, using Matt's lemon soap.

Staring at herself in the full-length mirror, she ran her hands down her body, hating it for its treacherous response to his demands. She looked tired, her blue eyes shadowed, her lips soft and red from his kisses, and here and there she could see faint marks on her skin where Matt had been a little too rough in his lovemaking.

She laughed mirthlessly at the idea of sex between them being described as lovemaking. Desire, perhaps; basic lust; but definitely not love, not any more.

Anna eyed herself critically. She was still slender, her skin smooth and firm though her breasts were a little heavier these days, and her stomach muscles not quite as taut. And she noticed a few tiny stretch-marks left over from her pregnancy...

She turned abruptly away from the mirror, shivering, feeling a familiar numbness creeping through her head, and, wrapping herself in a robe, went through to the kitchen.

There was the smell of bacon and coffee. Matt was by the stove cooking breakfast, dressed for the office in a light grey suit with a plastic apron over the top to protect it from splashes. He looked fit and healthy and handsome as he smiled at her across the table.

'Good morning. Did you sleep well?'

Anna felt suddenly shy, almost as though he were a stranger she'd allowed into her bed for the night. She nodded. 'Yes, thank you.'

He met her eyes, sighing as he said, 'Why so formal? Relax, Anna.'

She shrugged. What did he expect, for heaven's sake? They had been married a year and a half, and had once been so close they could read one another's thoughts, making words between them almost unnecessary. Now, his mind was closed to her, as hers was to him. They had just spent the night together yet she couldn't think of a thing to say to him.

'Sit down and eat,' he ordered, sliding a plate across to her.

Her stomach heaved at the sight of the food. 'Why are you doing this?' she demanded wearily. 'You know I don't eat breakfast.'

'Coffee, then?'

'Thanks.' He poured her a cup and her cold fingers curled gratefully around its warmth.

'How do you feel?' he asked, looking into her eyes.

Her pulses fluttered and, remembering her lack of control the night before, she felt angry and embarrassed.

He reached over the table and covered her hand with his. 'Don't look away from me, Anna,' he said softly. 'Don't be ashamed to admit you enjoyed our love-making. You never used to be ashamed.'

'I never used to be a lot of things,' she snapped. 'But circumstances change people, don't they, Matt?'

He flushed and his eyes slid away from hers. 'Only if you let them.'

'What do you expect from me?' she cried. 'Did you think I'd be the meek little wife and sit quietly by while you played around?' She shook her head in disbelief. 'Lord, you amaze me, you really do. You act as if being unfaithful is nothing at all.' She hadn't meant to say the words out loud, but they tumbled from her mouth like stones to lie heavily between them.

He pushed his chair back so violently that it fell with a clatter. 'So, we're back to that again, are we? I might have known. You're like a dog with a bone, aren't you, Anna? You just don't know when to let go! It's as though you've pushed a destruct button on our marriage and you're determined to keep your finger on it, come what may!'

She flinched before the anger in his voice, but held her ground. 'Don't you blame me!' she spat furiously. 'How dare you blame me?'

He stared at her helplessly, his arms wide as if in supplication, and she could see him fighting to control his anger as he arranged his face into the expression of weary patience which had become so bitterly familiar to her. 'You won't talk to me, Anna. We need to talk it through but you just shut me out.'

She looked away from the pain in his eyes. 'I...couldn't...I can't...' she said, feeling the threat of unspoken words like black fog on the edge of her mind.

'Don't you see?' he said gently. 'We have to talk about it some time.' He gripped her hands, holding them still. 'We must. We can't go on like this—it's been six months, dammit!'

He paced the kitchen restlessly while the forgotten food congealed on the plates and Anna, unable to help herself, began to cry, softly, hopelessly.

His fists clenched. 'Oh, lord, not more tears, please!'

Scrubbing at her wet cheeks with her hands, she snarled, 'I'm so sorry!'

He pushed his fingers through his hair, a helpless, irritated gesture she knew very well. 'I thought you were better. I told the doctor you weren't crying so much...'

'Been keeping notes on my progress, have you? "Today Anna actually smiled twice", or, "Today Anna didn't cry until after lunch"?'

'Don't be ridiculous, of course I haven't been keeping notes. I just think it's about time you pulled yourself together and stopped wallowing, that's all...'

'You callous bastard!' she cried, striking out at him with her fists. 'I hate you...I hate you!' She slid, sobbing, to the floor and crouched there, unable to hold back the pain that washed over her in drowning waves.

'Anna...Anna, I'm sorry.' He knelt beside her, holding her shaking body in his arms. 'Please, Anna, stop crying...I'm sorry.' His lips touched her hair and he pulled a handkerchief from his pocket to wipe her face. As he did so, something clattered on to the tiles; a small, brightly shining diamond earring.

Anna stared at it, recognising it as one of a pair Sarah had been wearing the evening before. She watched as Matt picked it up and dropped it back into his pocket.

'It's Sarah's,' he said carelessly. 'The clip has broken and I offered to take it to the jeweller for her this morning.'

Anna remembered the hot night, the gleam of Sarah's pearly skin contrasting with Matt's dark head, the sound of their laughter, Sarah's red nails against Matt's cheek, and she felt sick with grief and hatred.

'I saw you kissing her!' she muttered hoarsely. 'I saw you!' She beat at his chest with her small fists until he grasped her arms, squeezing painfully.

'Calm down, Anna, you'll make yourself ill!'

'Let go of me, you bastard!' She struggled to her feet, gasping for air, dizzy with rage and pain. 'I hate you!'

Matt swore softly and let her go, and she retreated until the table was between them.

'I'm sick of this. You'd better take a couple of your pills and lie down,' he said heavily.

'I don't want to take pills! I've had enough of your damned pills! That's what you want, isn't it? Keep little Anna nicely sedated so you can make it with your darling cousin Sarah!'

'For pity's sake, enough is enough!' Matt shouted.

'I agree. As far as you and I are concerned, enough is enough is the end!'

'What do you mean?'

'It means I'm leaving you. I want a divorce.' There, the words were out, shocking in their baldness, shocking Anna into silence as she saw his eyes turn cold, bleak, like hard grey slate.

He stared at her for several moments. 'After last night?'

'Especially after last night.' She looked away wearily. 'There's nothing left, don't you see?'

Laughing mirthlessly, he said, 'Nothing left? So, that was play-acting, was it? You're trying to tell me you were faking it when we made love?'

She shook her head. 'No, I wasn't faking anything and you know it, but it's all we have left and it's not enough. A good marriage needs more than sex.'

'Do you think I don't know that?'

'I don't know what you think, that's the trouble. You and I aren't on the same wavelength any more and there's no point in our staying together just to pick pieces out of one another...'

'Anna, you're tired,' he said placatingly. 'You'll feel differently when you've had time to think about it...'

'I've done enough thinking to last me a lifetime, mostly when I was alone. When you were away on business, or working late with Sarah, remember?'

He flushed, unable to deny the truth of her words.

'I can't take the way we are any longer,' she continued. 'You and Sarah, and the company——'

'The company?' He rounded on her. 'I work for the company, Anna. I have to earn a living and I haven't noticed you turning down the comforts my position has given you. All the clothes and jewellery, and the holidays abroad. Or perhaps you would have preferred it if we'd eked out a grubby existence in some squalid shack?'

'Don't exaggerate, you know what I mean,' she said with a sigh.

'No, I don't, so tell me.'

She faced him squarely. 'All right, I will. I mean the hypocritical attitudes of the people we have to mix with, the grasping ambition and back-stabbing, and the way people think nothing of bending their marriage vows to suit expediency, and possible promotion.'

'Are you suggesting that I . . . ?'

Anna shrugged. 'If the cap fits, as they say.'

'I don't need that kind of a leg up, my love,' he sneered. 'I get my promotion through my own ability to do the job better than anyone else.'

'Plus the fact that you're the chairman's nephew.'

Matt turned away from her in disgust. 'I've had enough of this.' He slipped into his jacket, glancing at his watch. 'I have a meeting in half an hour and if I don't leave now I'll be late.' He looked at her from beneath his brows. 'Have some rest, and when I get back tonight we'll try and talk this thing through calmly and sensibly, OK?'

She didn't reply. There was no point, because she didn't plan to be there when he got back.

The doors opened and Anna emerged from the Customs hall into the arrivals area at Gatwick Airport. Dressed in blue cotton jeans and shirt, she looked far younger than her twenty-three years, so much so that a member of the airport staff smiled kindly at her and asked if she was being met.

She shook her head and thanked him and he went away. She hesitated a moment, feeling panic as the crowd jostled past her. What was she doing here alone? The anger and pain which had driven her to fly home from New York so precipitately had ebbed a little now, and she could only think of Matt coming back to the apartment to find her gone.

Would he drive to the airport in the hope of stopping her? Unlikely. He had once told her he'd never run after any woman. But Anna wasn't just any woman. She was his wife. That was supposed to make a difference, wasn't it?

She shrugged, telling herself that Matt, and what he might or might not do, wasn't her concern any more.

The arrivals hall was filled with people and Anna felt terribly alone amid the bustle. It was hot and her shirt stuck between her shoulder-blades. Her case felt heavy, though there wasn't much inside it. She had been in too much of a hurry to pack everything, too eager to get away, to run from the pain of knowing that Matt didn't love her.

But she should have realised that she couldn't outrun the pain. It was part of her, a vast, empty, aching part of her.

She felt a hand touch her arm. A voice spoke her name and she turned to see the bland, smiling face of Matt's mother's chauffeur and forced an answering smile to her lips. 'Hello, Butlin. I didn't expect to be met.'

Butlin's face was expressionless as he said, 'Mr Matthew cabled, madam. He suggested I collect you and see you safely back to Ashley Park.'

No way, thought Anna. Her mother-in-law's contemptuous sympathy would be more than she could take right now. But Matt had cabled, which meant he knew she had gone.

'Thanks, anyway,' she said coolly, 'but I won't be going to Ashley Park. I'd be grateful for a lift into London, though. I need to pick up a few things from the cottage and then I'm going home for a while.'

Somewhere inside herself she was amazed she could sound so normal as she took in Butlin's slightly incredulous expression.

'Home, madam?'

'Yes, to Yorkshire.'

'Very good, madam.'

Clearly the chauffeur considered Yorkshire to be on a par with the North Pole. He took Anna's case and ushered her towards the exit, his back stiff with disapproval.

So what? she thought. Half an hour and she need never see him again. She need never see any of them again—her mother-in-law, Matt's snobbish sisters, all the numerous aunts, uncles and cousins who had looked with such amusement at his choice of a bride, their united disapproval carefully concealed behind a façade of polite interest.

But then it hadn't mattered because Matt had loved her. He found his mother's relentless snobbery a huge joke and all his love and laughter had protected Anna from possible hurt. Though when they were first married she hadn't needed any protection. She had been strong, filled with confidence in both herself and his love.

That time seemed light years away to her now as she stared out at the fresh green English countryside flashing past the car window. She closed her eyes, feeling the ache of tiredness behind the lids. How long was it since she'd had a decent night's sleep? Six months. Six months of misery and loss, and heartbreak for what might have been...

Her baby, their baby, would have been six months old now and her arms still ached for him. She still burned with sorrow and resentment that it had been her child, her small, perfect son whose life had been snuffed out within hours of his birth.

A malformed heart, the paediatrician had told them regretfully. Anna had held him before he died, a small human being with Matt's features in miniature. They had named him Daniel. She had looked at him, felt him warm against her breast, and love, like a possessive tide, had filled her, a sharp, almost painful surge of feeling overflowing from her body to surround and protect him.

But it hadn't been enough, and when they had taken him from her the sense of loss and emptiness had been unbearable, was still unbearable.

Of course they had given her bottles of pills to take, tranquillisers and sleeping-tablets. The bottles lay untouched in the bottom of her handbag. She had refused to take them, not wanting to blunt the edge of her grief and pretend it didn't exist. Her baby had lived, she had felt him move inside her body, part of her. Coming to terms with his death was something she would have to do without resorting to drugs.

Butlin dropped her outside the pretty mews cottage where she and Matt had lived since their marriage. Anna was quite fond of the little house with its antique furniture and pictures, the off-white carpet and green velvet curtains. With her large collection of green plants and the little trees in pots outside the front door, she could almost imagine she was in the country. She'd miss living here, but she knew she couldn't stay. It wasn't hers any more.

Anna slowly climbed the spiral staircase to their bedroom. She ran her fingers along the satin surface of her dressing-table and Matt's face looked out at her from the silver frame beside her jewel box.

She stared hungrily at the features of the man she had married, had lived with for a year and a half, seeing high cheekbones and a strong, square jaw; the clearly defined mouth curved in a secret, sensual smile; the eyes gazing straight into the camera, dark, gleaming and slightly cynical, fringed with thick lashes; ironically curved brows and glossy black hair springing back from a wide, intelligent forehead.

Anna shivered. She could feel his presence in the room with her. This room where they had slept together, made love, held each other close. There was still the faint smell of his aftershave and the pain inside her was suddenly like a live thing, burning through the numbness, twisting, tearing, and she wrapped her arms around her body, whimpering, squeezing her eyes tightly shut against the memories that crowded her mind.

But she could still see his face, see him in their bed; smooth brown skin, wide shoulders and a muscled chest lightly furred with dark hair, a hard flat belly, lean hips and long taut thighs.

And his arms reaching out for her, that devastating smile, and the sleepy, sexy look in his dark grey eyes. Anna trembled helplessly, remembering, loving him, wanting him.

She lay down on the bed and clutched his pillow to her, pressing her face into its softness, breathing his scent from the crisp fresh linen as memories surged through the barriers she had erected in her mind...

CHAPTER TWO

AFTERWARDS, Anna realised she might never have met Matt if Webster, her gran's white cat, hadn't taken it in his head to wander off one day in June, and if she hadn't gone into the grounds of Crossthwaite Manor to look for him...

The manor had burned down long before and the grounds were securely fenced against intruders, but Anna knew where there were small gaps in the wire and had come armed with a scythe, which she used to slash her way through the nettles growing head-high around what was left of the old house, calling the cat's name as she went.

She climbed the broken steps to the doorway and peered inside. What had once been an elegant entrance hall was open to the sky and littered with fallen masonry.

Then she saw a cat. Not Webster, but a thin, sharp-faced tabby staring suspiciously at her from behind a clump of nettles. She was about to step through the doorway when a voice behind her said,

'What do you think you're doing, lad? Come out of there right now!'

The tabby cat leapt away. Anna froze. The voice had authority and she was trespassing. She turned, squaring her shoulders defiantly; after all, she hadn't done any harm.

A man stood at the bottom of the steps. He put his hands on his hips and looked her up and down. He wore denims and appeared lean and taut, and tough. He had black hair and his eyes were a peculiar grey, slate-dark and penetrating. Anna felt herself shiver beneath his steady gaze.

His mouth curved into a smile. 'You're a girl,' he said, surprised.

'So I've been told,' she replied pertly.

Shrugging, he indicated her scruffy jeans and checked shirt. 'Well, you look like a boy from the back, especially with that cropped haircut. Though now I come to think about it, no boy I ever saw had such a curvy backside,' he added with a grin.

Anna felt herself blush annoyingly. He was standing very close, looking up at her, the top of his head on a level with her breasts. She saw his eyes flick over her and, even though the shape of her body was all but hidden beneath her baggy shirt, she had the sudden, self-conscious urge to hide herself behind her hands. 'If you've done passing remarks perhaps you'll move out of the way so I can get down.'

'Of course.' He put out a hand to help her. She ignored it, jumped and turned her ankle painfully. Tears of frustration filled her eyes, which weren't helped at all by his scornful laughter.

'Serves you right,' he said callously. 'What are you doing in here, anyway? Don't you know it's private property?'

'Of course I know,' she muttered between clenched teeth. 'There's a notice ten feet high saying, "Private. Keep Out." There's nothing wrong with *my* eyesight!'

'So, what are you doing in here?'

'I might ask you the same question. Are you poaching?'

'Certainly not, you cheeky young madam. I came to look the place over for a prospective buyer, if you must know.'

Anna stared at him incredulously. 'Somebody's buying this place?'

'Perhaps.'

She looked around at the desolation. 'What for? It's a ruin.'

'Nosy little thing, aren't you?' he laughed.

'No, just interested. After all, I live just along the road. I like to know what's going on.'

'Hmm.' He looked at her from beneath his brows. 'How did you get in, anyway?'

'Through the fence,' she admitted.

'Is anyone with you?'

Without stopping to think, Anna shook her head. 'No, I was looking for my cat.'

He sighed. 'OK, you'd better show me where you broke in.'

She could tell he didn't believe her about the cat. He fell into step beside her as they walked back towards the trees, where the path she'd made was clearly visible.

His movements had the graceful economy of a jungle animal, lithe, soft-footed, and Anna felt fear touch her skin. Supposing he was a criminal, or an escaped lunatic, and here she was alone with him.

Then he swore under his breath and she turned to see him rubbing his forearm.

'Lord, these nettles are vicious. You must be stung up to hell.'

'A little,' she replied, and passed him a dock leaf. 'Here, rub it with this, it's supposed to help.'

Anna felt herself relaxing fractionally, unable to imagine a desperate criminal making such a fuss over a simple nettle sting, though she couldn't feel any sympathy for him when her ankle was throbbing more with every step, making walking an agony.

They reached the gap in the fence and she wriggled through on her hands and knees, uncomfortably aware of her undignified posture. He squeezed his bulk after her, tearing a hole in his shirt in the process, which brought forth more swear-words.

'OK,' he said threateningly, 'how many more of you are there?'

'How many more what?' she asked blankly.

'Kids, of course. I suppose you hide out in here now it's the school holidays.'

He thought she was a schoolgirl, she realised, amused. Though she knew she must look much younger than her twenty-one years, in the tatty jeans and tennis shoes, and hardly any figure to speak of under the baggy shirt. And who was she to disillusion him?

She smiled, shaking her head. 'No, there's only me. I told you, I'm looking for my cat. You don't think I'd come in here for fun, do you? This place gives me the creeps.' Forgetting her ankle, she put her full weight on it, gasping at the sudden jolt of pain.

'Here, let me have a look at that,' he said at once. He almost pushed her down on to the grass verge beside the road and lifted her foot in its disreputable shoe, cradling her heel in one hand while the fingers of the other gently probed the delicate bones. 'Where does it hurt?'

She reached down to show him the place and his hand momentarily covered hers. His touch was warm and hard and Anna snatched her hand away as if she'd been burned. He slanted a glance at her from beneath his brows, his eyes lingering on the V of smooth skin exposed at the open neck of her shirt.

Anna felt naked, as though her clothes had suddenly become transparent. He was too close. She could smell his faint masculine scent, musky, disturbing. She trembled, breathless, her mouth dry as she became aware of an almost unbearable surge of excitement.

His fingers caressed her ankle and the bottom of her leg and she quivered deliciously. His hand stilled and she looked up and met his eyes, saw questions in their dark gaze.

Then he laughed and, standing, hauled her to her feet.

'Come on, girl-child, you're not playing games with me, I'm way out of your league. Try it on someone nearer your own age.'

'What do you mean?' she demanded, feeling her face grow hot.

'You know damned well what I mean, so you can cut out the wide-eyed innocent act because I'm not falling for it.'

Anna stared at him. What did he think she was, for heaven's sake, some kind of teenaged temptress out to snare him? Aloud she said, 'You have a high opinion of yourself, don't you?'

'No,' he replied, shrugging. 'I just know women and how their devious little minds work, that's all.'

'Really?' Her voice was loaded with indifference as she bent to retrieve her bike from the ditch. 'Well, much as I'd love to stay and continue this fascinating conversation, I'm afraid I must be going now, Mr—er——?'

'Tennant...Matthew Tennant,' he supplied, still grinning.

'How do you do, Mr Tennant? And goodbye,' she said coldly, and, mounting the bike, was about to ride away when his hand touched her arm.

'You haven't told me your name.'

'Does it matter?'

'Well, it might,' he said, laughing. 'You said something about a cat?'

She'd forgotten all about poor old Webster. 'Oh, yes, he's a white Persian,' she told him, nodding towards Crossthwaite Manor. 'Have you seen one in there?'

'The place is overrun with cats, but I can't say I remember seeing a white Persian among them. Mind you, all cats look alike to me.'

'Well, they would, wouldn't they?' Anna said sweetly. 'Why don't you invest in a pair of glasses, or maybe a white stick?'

'Very funny. Watch it, kid!' he warned. 'Has your cat been missing long?'

'Three days. My gran is going frantic. Webster's getting on a bit, you see, and he's never gone off like this before.'

'Good lord, what a weird name for a cat.'

'It's after Webster Booth, you know, the singer,' Anna explained.

He laughed again. 'A bit before my time, love. But I'll have a look around for your cat.'

'Thanks, that's very kind of you. Goodbye, Mr Tennant.' She started to ride away only to stop again as he called after her.

'You'd better tell me your name and address in case I find him.'

'Oh...yes, of course. I'm Anna Marshall and I live at the mill.' She pointed back down the lane to where chimneys were just visible among the trees.

'How do you do, Miss Marshall?' he said mockingly. 'Bye for now.'

Anna rode home deep in thought. The man, Matthew Tennant, was different somehow, even dangerous, though she didn't know why she should feel that way about him. She guessed him to be in his early thirties, certainly not much younger. He had that unmistakable air of experience and self-possession that a younger man wouldn't have.

She shivered as she recalled the arrogant way he had stood over her and the striking good looks. Fascinating, enigmatic ... different.

Anna laughed at herself, dismissing her thoughts as silly nonsense. She was sensible, level-headed, everyone said so. Suddenly to go all soft inside over a man she'd only just met was too ridiculous for words, yet all that day she found herself listening for the front doorbell, willing it to ring, and for the caller to be Matthew Tennant.

Yet when it did finally ring, at seven o'clock in the evening, it was with no real surprise that she saw him waiting in the front porch with a cardboard box under one arm. It was as if she'd known all along that he would come.

'Hello,' he said, smiling. 'I think I've found Webster.'

'How marvellous! Do come in.' She pulled the door wide and he stepped into the hall, ducking his head to avoid the lintel. In the sitting-room he unfastened the box and a grubby, disgruntled Webster hopped out.

Anna's grandmother swept the animal into her arms with a cry of joy. 'Where on earth did you find him?'

'Over at the manor, making love to a very scruffy-looking tabby cat,' he told her with a grin.

Anna stared at him. 'But he can't ... I mean he's been ... well, you know,' she finished lamely, feeling a blush creep up her face.

He laughed. 'Poor old Webster, he has my sympathy.'

'Do sit down, Mr ...?' her grandmother interposed briskly.

'Matthew Tennant,' he said.

'Ah, yes, Anna did mention meeting you. I'm Kate Marshall,' she added, holding out her free hand. 'Well,

Mr Tennant, I'm very grateful to you for finding Webster.' She eyed the truant animal fondly.

'No problem. I'm glad I was able to help,' he said. 'And call me Matt, please.'

'Of course. Can I offer you a drink? Tea or coffee, or perhaps you'd prefer something a little stronger. I have a bottle of excellent malt whisky.'

'Coffee will do fine, thanks.'

Kate went to get the coffee and give Webster his supper, leaving Anna to entertain their guest.

'Thank you so much for finding Webster,' she said. 'Gran's been going out of her mind with worry.'

Matt laughed. 'He didn't think much to my idea of bringing him home. He seemed quite happy with his love-affair among the ruins.'

'At his age he should be ashamed of himself.'

'He was probably seeking his lost youth. It happens to the best of us in the end.' He glanced around the room, taking in the low beamed ceiling, the white plastered walls which were uneven with age, and the bright rugs on polished oak floorboards. 'This is a lovely old house. Have you lived here long?'

'Since I was six,' she told him. 'Though the mill has been in our family for three hundred years.'

'I saw a sign on the gate which said "Mill Pottery". You make pots?'

'Gran does. She supplies most of the gift shops in the Yorkshire Dales.'

'Sounds interesting. I suppose you'll join the business when you leave school?'

Anna suppressed a giggle and decided it was time to change the subject. 'Is someone really going to rebuild the manor?' she asked.

'Possibly. The company I work for is looking for a site in the country for a new laboratory. Crossthwaite Manor is only one of many we're considering.'

'A laboratory? What for?' Anna demanded. 'Not experiments on animals, I hope?'

Matt laughed, a hearty male sound that seemed startlingly out of place in Kate Marshall's sitting-room. 'No, not animal experiments, and from the look on your face I think it's probably just as well. I bet you'd be the first to picket the place with a banner.'

'You're darn right, I would,' Anna said emphatically. 'We don't want anything like that in Crossthwaite, thank you very much. What do you do?' she asked, her voice filled with suspicion.

'I'm a geologist. I work for Barratt Oil.'

Anna recognised the name at once: an international company with its name blazoned on a chain of filling stations nationwide.

'I thought geologists studied rocks and things, not prospective building sites,' she remarked.

'I suppose I'm what you might call a jack of all trades. I go where my uncle sends me.'

'Your uncle?'

'James Barratt.'

She raised her brows. 'Wow, I'm impressed,' she said mockingly.

'I thought you might be,' he replied with a grin, and leaned back comfortably against the sofa cushions, watching her.

He wore black cord jeans that fitted sleekly to his lean hips, and a black sweatshirt with the sleeves pushed back to reveal tanned forearms. He was aggressively masculine, and Anna was suddenly breathless, feeling pinioned beneath his gaze. She couldn't think of a thing to say. How silly to feel so confused, yet so tinglingly alive, all at the same time.

She glanced away and knew she was blushing. Where was Gran with the coffee? Any second now she'd start babbling about the weather and he'd really think her a fool.

'I passed this place the other day and wondered who was fortunate enough to live here,' he said into the taut silence.

'Really? Are you staying locally, then?'

'With friends near Leeds,' he said. He was completely at ease, relaxed, and probably waiting for her to make some intelligent remark. But it was as if her brain had suddenly ceased to function, leaving only blankness, and an overwhelming awareness of him filling the room; his eyes, his smile, his hands resting loosely in his lap, and the faint scent of his aftershave, subtle and disturbing to her senses.

She stood up, feeling as though her hands and feet had just grown three sizes, and blurted, 'I'll go and see where Gran has got to with that coffee.'

In the hall she pressed her palms to her burning cheeks. Kate Marshall came towards her carrying a tray laden with coffee things, and a large chocolate cake.

Anna looked at the cake, then at her grandmother. 'That's a bit over the top, isn't it?' she whispered.

'One must be hospitable, dear. Besides, he did bring Webster back.' She pushed at the sitting-room door with her hip. 'Where are you off to, anyway?'

'The bathroom,' Anna lied, and hurried upstairs.

In the sanctuary of her bedroom she dragged a comb through her hair, cursing the curls which refused to be smoothed flat, and eyed herself critically, wishing she had more of a figure. She pulled her shirt tighter across her breasts, and with a grimace, realised it only emphasised their smallness. Better leave it loose and at least maintain an air of mystery.

She chewed her lips and arranged them into what was supposed to be a sexy pout, then, filled with a sudden sense of the ridiculous, began to giggle.

'Sexy you are not, Anna Marshall,' she told her reflection wryly, and shook her head. What an idiot! As if it mattered what she looked like. And why on earth should she worry about impressing a man she'd probably never see again? And one, besides, who thought she was still a schoolgirl.

So, with her feelings well under control, she went back downstairs and found her grandmother happily chatting with Matt Tennant, who was already on his second slice of cake.

Anna helped herself to coffee and returned to her footstool.

'This cake is delicious,' he said. 'Did you make it?'

Anna shook her head. 'No, I don't cook much.'

'I thought all girls did cooking at school.'

'That's a typically sexist attitude,' she retorted. 'Besides, I didn't say I can't, just that I don't. Just because I happened to be born female, it doesn't follow that I have to be labelled "domestic chores only"!'

Matt raised his brows, clearly amused. 'What happens when you grow up and get married?'

That stung and she glared at him. 'When and if I decide to get married, I'll find myself a man whose macho image doesn't depend on having me waiting on him hand and foot!'

'There are some things men can't do, you know,' he pointed out. 'Personally, I find aggressively liberated females a definite turn-off.'

Anna shot him a look which she hoped told him clearly that she didn't care much of a damn what he found! He was evidently nothing but a male chauvinist who thought a woman should be either in his kitchen or his bed. He looked the type.

'You'll feel differently when you grow up,' he said patronisingly, laughing.

Anna could have hit him. Why did he have this effect on her? She felt all screwed up inside, edgy, nervous, rather like the Christmas Eve feeling she'd had as a child, only more so. She wished Matthew Tennant would go. She didn't like the unsettling effect he had on her nerves, making her feel ill at ease, like a cat with its fur rubbed the wrong way. She didn't like the way his strange eyes flicked over her, arousing uncomfortable emotions, a soft warmth inside her, a shivery sensation on her skin.

Most of all she didn't like the message in those glances that told her he knew exactly how she was feeling, and, when he finally stood up to leave, she was appalled to hear her grandmother inviting him to lunch the following Sunday.

'Thanks, I'd love to,' he said. He turned to Anna. 'Will you be able to show me over the mill on Sunday? I'd be very interested to see it all.'

'I won't be here,' she said evenly. 'It's my turn at the shop on Sunday.'

'Only until lunchtime, dear,' said Kate, adding, 'You must look in at Anna's gift shop while you're in Crossthwaite, Matt. Perhaps you noticed it—Treasures, on Main Street?'

'You mean that quaint little place with the bow windows? I was in there the other day looking for a present for my mother's birthday. Isn't that a coincidence?'

'Isn't it just?' Anna sighed, unable to meet his eyes.

'Have you been doing that kind of thing long?' he asked, his voice filled with laughter.

'Since I finished college last year,' she told him.

'That would make you around twenty?'

'Twenty-one, actually,' she said shortly, looking up to meet his gaze, which had suddenly become decidedly predatory.

'Imagine that,' he said softly. 'I'd never have guessed it. Well, goodbye for now, Miss Marshall. I'll look forward to seeing you on Sunday.'

'I won't be here,' she said firmly. There was no way she was hanging around to give Matthew Tennant a guided tour of the mill, and whatever else took his fancy!

His answering smile was wicked. 'Perhaps you'll change your plans.'

Something lurched inside her and her knees trembled. Damn the man! Why did he make her feel this way?

She shook her head, saying, 'I doubt it. Goodnight, Mr Tennant.'

The phone was ringing! Anna fought her way through layers of sleep, still so deep in her dream that for several moments she was totally disorientated. She peeled open gritty eyelids and stared stupidly at the phone by the bed, before reaching out to pick up the receiver.

'Yes?' The word came out as a croak past a tongue that felt like a piece of blotting-paper in her mouth.

'Anna?'

'Yes.' Her voice was stronger now, and her pulses increased to a steady throb as she heard Matt on the line.

'You sound odd. Are you all right?'

'I was asleep,' she said defensively.

'In the middle of the afternoon?'

'Jet lag.'

'I see.' He sounded suspicious, not angry as she had expected. 'Why are you at the cottage? I arranged for you to go to Ashley and stay with Mother till I get back. She sent the car for you, didn't she?'

'Yes.'

'So, why are you in London all by yourself, darling?'

Anna couldn't bear the weary patience in his voice. It was better when he was angry. She could deal with his anger. 'I couldn't face your mother.'

'I'm not surprised. Of all the damn fool things for you to do, this takes first prize—but you don't have to worry, I didn't tell Mother anything much, just that you were tired and needed a change.'

'That was big of you,' Anna said. 'Why the sudden concern for my feelings?'

'At this point *your* feelings don't come into it, love. I just want to avoid any unnecessary speculation among the family,' he retorted.

'Why not tell them the truth? They'll have to know eventually.'

'I'm hoping it won't come to that, Anna. Listen, I'm catching the next available flight to London, so stay put and we'll talk when I get there, OK?'

'I don't want you to come.' Anna was trembling. She didn't want to face Matt until she'd had a chance to get herself together. She was too vulnerable right now.

'What do you mean, you don't want me to come?'

'Exactly what I said. I told you already, I've left you and I'm not coming back. I shall be seeing my lawyer about a divorce.'

There was a long pause and Anna listened to her own heartbeats, appalled by the baldness of her words.

'Just like that?' he said finally.

'Yes,' she whispered. Then she heard music and someone else talking and knew he wasn't alone.

'Look, I can't talk right now, but I'll be with you as soon as I can get a flight. Stay put and don't do anything stupid.'

There was a click as the connection was broken. Anna rolled on to her back and stared at the ceiling. What did he mean by telling her not to do anything stupid? Did he think she was likely to throw herself into the Thames or something?

And who was he with? Probably darling Sarah. She squeezed her eyes shut, imagining, and hatred churned her stomach; hatred, jealousy and a bitter sense of loss.

Matt stared at the dead phone while across the room Sarah stabbed impatiently at the selector buttons on the television remote control.

'Sarah, do you mind? If you want to watch TV go and do it somewhere else, there's a good girl.'

'I don't want to watch TV. There's nothing on but game shows and soap operas anyway. But I have to do something. You won't talk to me.'

'I do have rather a lot on my mind right now.'

'Oh, for heaven's sake, you're not pining for the wee wifey, are you?' She uncoiled her elegant self from her place on the floor and came over to him, slender and beautiful in peacock-blue harem pants and a matching silk shirt that did little to hide the fact that she was naked underneath. She leaned over him and her hair swept his cheek as she nibbled his ear.

'Come on, lover, I can think of better things to do than moon over lost causes.'

With his eyes fixed on Anna's picture on his desk-top, he pushed Sarah away, shaking his head. 'Give me a break, Sal, please.'

Her face cold with temper, she flounced across to the sofa and picked up her jacket and bag. 'I'm running out of patience with you, Matt. Lord knows I've given you enough time to get Anna out of your system...'

Matt looked at her, his expression hard. 'I've heard enough, Sarah. Just do me a favour and get out of here—now!'

She pouted at him. 'Are you coming to Malibu with me, or do you intend to go running off after *her*?'

'I think you know the answer to that,' he said quietly.

She shrugged. 'You're a fool, Matt. Anna couldn't even give you a healthy child!' And with that last cruel barb, she slammed out of the room.

Matthew sighed and rubbed at the tense muscles in the back of his neck. Why was he going after Anna when she'd made it perfectly clear she didn't want him?

He stared through the window at the busy New York skyline, and thought of an English garden in June, with the scent of lavender and roses, the sound of water trickling over mossy stones, and the lazy drone of bees.

And Anna standing before the background of an old drystone wall, her blue eyes screwed shut against the brightness of the sunlight, sunlight that turned her short, baby-soft curls to gold. And Anna's laughter...

He pushed himself restlessly to his feet. It was a long time since he had heard Anna laugh, and he tasted the bitterness of disillusion in his mouth, mingled with frustration and anger that she had shut him out of her mind and heart, and had the nerve to walk out on him, just like that.

He recalled the uncomfortable conversation he'd had with his uncle earlier this morning.

'It won't do, my boy,' James had said. 'You're my nephew, after all. The rest of them look to you to set an example.' He'd thumped the shiny desk-top, making the antique silver inkstand rattle. 'The Barratt image is family togetherness, so it's best you get it through to that little girl you married and let's have no more of this separation nonsense!'

Matthew looked at his uncle with dislike. 'My marriage is none of your damned business!' he snapped harshly.

'That's where you're wrong, boy. While your mother relies on me to support her extravagant lifestyle in that bloody great house, you'll dance to my tune and like it!'

Leaning forward over the desk, Matt faced his uncle, his eyes cold with rage. 'Don't threaten me, Uncle James,' he said. 'My father owned half this company, remember!'

James Barratt's mouth twisted with contempt. 'Your father was a weak fool who took his own life when the going got tough. When I bought his half of the company from your mother it was worthless and you know it. I've made Barratts' what it is today and don't *you* forget it!'

But Matt had never backed down before his uncle and he wasn't about to start now. He faced him squarely, his voice soft with menace as he said, 'I've given you twelve years of my life, so I figure we're more than even and, I repeat, my marriage is none of your damned business! And if you want my resignation, you can have it right now!'

James had smiled and blustered as Matt had known he would. 'There's no need for that, my boy,' he'd said. 'I'm sure you and Anna will manage to sort things out between you.'

Matt frowned. The trouble was, he and his uncle were too much alike. This morning's quarrel was only one of many they'd had over the years, and Matt was very well aware that, if it hadn't been for the fact that he loved his job, he'd have told James Barratt to go to hell long ago.

His thoughts were interrupted by the politely re-
strained buzzing of the telephone. He lifted the receiver
and a disembodied voice on the line told him he was
booked on a flight to Heathrow early the next morning.

He smiled grimly at Anna's photograph on his desk.
'I'll be in London tomorrow morning, Anna, my girl,
and you'd better be there...!'

CHAPTER THREE

ANNA dressed in jeans and a T-shirt and went down to make coffee in the immaculate little kitchen. She couldn't think which day it was and had to look at the calendar. Wednesday. Their daily would be coming in to open up the house ready for their return from New York on Friday, but she'd be gone by then.

She took a notebook and pen from her bag and made a list of things to do. This was positive action and writing everything down made it more clear in her mind. She was a naturally tidy person and creating order by listing small tasks helped keep her thoughts from the greater chaos of her broken marriage.

When she had finished she stared at the list, which dealt with practical things, like the transfer of money from her London account, and the removal of her personal belongings back to Crossthwaite. She thought longingly of her grandmother and the mill, and picked up the phone.

It rang for a long time before her gran finally answered, sounding breathless.

'I was in the garden,' she said. 'Anna, is that you? I thought you were in New York until next weekend.'

'I came back early,' Anna told her, not wanting to give explanations over the phone.

'Is Matt with you?'

'No... he's still over there. Listen, is it all right if I come and stay with you for a while?'

'Of course, darling, you know you don't have to ask. When will you be arriving?'

'This evening. I'll get a taxi from the station so don't worry about meeting the train.'

There was a brief pause, then Kate said, 'Is everything all right, Anna?'

'Yes...yes, fine. I'll see you later.'

By four-thirty she had finished her packing. The case she was taking with her stood ready in the hall. Not much really, she thought. Just a few personal items: clothes, her embroidery things, the photograph of Matt in its silver frame, and her jewel box containing the pieces which had been her mother's.

The valuable jewellery Matt had given her was securely locked in their safety deposit box at the bank, and there it could stay as far as Anna was concerned. She took only her locket, her wedding-ring and the photograph. She wanted nothing more from him.

Half an hour remained before she must leave to catch her train to Leeds. She prowled the cottage, going from room to room, feeling already as if she didn't belong. Yet she had been so happy here, with Matt. She had loved him so much.

She went into the kitchen to wash her coffee things and tidy up, and, filling the bowl with hot water, plunged her hands into it, then paused, her eyes closed as she found herself thinking of that first Sunday Matt had come to Mill House. She smiled softly, remembering. She hadn't realised it at the time, but he'd had her love, even then...

She had told him she'd be out, but of course she'd been there waiting when he rang the doorbell, though not about to give in gracefully, no way! She was aggressive, prickly, acutely conscious of his every movement.

Seeing her there he smiled knowingly and said, 'Hello. So you changed your mind, then?'

'I beg your pardon?' She hated his arrogant assumption that she'd stayed at home on his account.

'You did say you'd be out today,' he reminded her.

'I did, didn't I?' She shrugged. 'So, I changed my mind, but don't let it go to your head.'

He laughed mockingly and she felt dislike boiling up inside her, all the more frustrating because she couldn't think of a single thing to say.

She found herself watching Matt covertly. He was wearing well-cut brown trousers, a cream silk shirt and soft suede jacket. His dark hair was brushed back in a casually long style, and he looked lean and fit, with a hard elegance which intrigued her, yet also made her a little afraid.

His eyes flicked over her and it was as if he were actually touching her skin, sending quivers of something like excitement along her nerve-endings.

'Do I get my guided tour of the mill?' he asked eventually, smiling.

She glanced at her watch. 'Yes, if you come now. Doug's picking me up in a couple of hours and I have to change.'

Anna felt intensely vulnerable alone with him as they crossed the cobbled mill yard. Without quite knowing why, she had made an effort with her clothes and was wearing a dress for once, in cool blue cotton with a gypsy frill at the scooped neck and a full skirt. Her hair curled softly and she had used mascara and a touch of blue shadow on her eyes.

She felt feminine and pretty and one level of her mind revelled in the admiration she saw in Matt's dark eyes, while, confusingly, another part of her despised her efforts to impress him.

Matt smiled, rather warily she thought. 'Would it be too curious of me to ask who Doug is?'

'He's a friend,' she said.

'Boyfriend?'

'Just a friend,' she repeated. 'His mother went to school with Gran, and I've known him all my life. We go out together occasionally. Nothing heavy.'

'Good,' said Matt with a satisfied nod.

She didn't stop to analyse what he might mean by that as she unlocked the door to the mill. Inside it was dark and dusty, with light from the small-paned windows obscured by layers of dirt and cobwebs. Matt pushed back all the doors and fingers of sunlight reached into dim corners, revealing piles of disused junk and old machinery.

Careless of the dirt on his clothes, Matt poked about among it all, talking knowledgeably about main shafts and crown-wheels.

'This is magnificent,' he enthused. 'I wish I could have seen it working.' He gazed up at the high roof; slates were missing and birds had nested among the rafters. There was a strong damp smell and they could hear the soft rush of water beneath their feet.

'For a geologist, you seem to know a lot about mills,' Anna commented.

'I'm interested in old buildings. I like old things,' he said simply.

That surprised her. He didn't appear to be the type to care about the past and its traditions. After all he worked in an industry that was essentially of today and tomorrow, but when she voiced this opinion out loud he laughed.

'I work for Barratt Oil to earn my living but it's not my whole life. Sometimes I escape and find little out-of-the-way places like this to explore.' He waved his arms wide. 'This is the real thing. You can imagine real people living and working here.'

Anna smiled, feeling a new shared interest with him that was almost a meeting of minds, a blending of thought. Which was odd—after all, this man was a stranger to her. She might find him nice to look at, pleasant to talk to, but he was still a stranger.

Even so, she was aware of a deep sense of contentment, and when Matt took her hand she didn't pull away, but let her fingers curl around his, loving the hard contact of his warm skin against hers.

Outside they paused beside a locked door in the corner of the yard, where the mill buildings joined the house.

'This is my workroom,' she told him. 'Do you want to see inside?'

He smiled. 'Yes, please. That is if you don't mind.'

She opened the door and he stepped back to allow her to precede him and she felt the light touch of his hand at her waist, seeming to burn her flesh through the thin cotton dress. She moved hastily into the room, confused by a sudden desire to feel him close to her, feeling again that strange intense pleasure in his company.

The little room was filled with sunlight from a large window shining on the chintz-covered chair in which sat her old and battered teddy-bear. Several shelves were filled with books, and her embroidery frame was angled to catch the light. On it was a completed piece of work: a picture of anemones done in silk on linen; glowing, jewel-bright colours made the flowers seem almost real enough to touch.

Matt stared down at the picture and gently traced the delicate outline of a leaf with his forefinger. 'You're a very talented lady,' he said at last, with something that might have been awe in his voice.

Anna felt warm inside, a brightness filling her with pleasure at his compliment. 'Thank you.'

'You can earn a living doing this kind of thing?' he asked.

'This, and the shop,' she told him. 'Lucy and I started Treasures last year and so far we've done rather well, selling local handicrafts to the tourists.'

'Lucy?'

'Lucy Howard. You must have seen her when you were in the shop—the girl with bright red hair?' Matt nodded, and Anna continued, 'We were at art college together. She makes the most wonderful silver jewellery.'

'So, you decided to pool your talents and set up in business?'

Anna nodded. 'It seemed the logical thing to do. There are so many people needing a market for their craftware that we felt it was worth the risk.'

'You never mentioned your parents,' he remarked.

'They're both dead,' she said shortly.

'Oh, lord, I'm sorry. Forgive me for being so clumsy.'

'That's all right, it was a long time ago.'

'You must miss them very much.'

Anna glanced at him. He sounded as if he really cared. 'Yes, I do miss them, though not as badly as at first. They were both drowned in a boating accident when I was six.'

'You poor kid!' He sounded almost angry.

Anna smiled. 'There's no need to feel sorry for me. As I said, it was a long time ago and I've had Gran, and in a way it was worse for her because Dad was her only child. I can't think of anything more terrible than losing your own child.'

'So, your grandmother brought you up?'

'Yes, we're very close,' Anna said simply.

'I envy you.'

Anna was surprised. 'Why?'

Shrugging, he said, 'I don't know. Maybe I envy you the closeness you share with your grandmother.'

'What about your own parents?' she asked.

He laughed bitterly. 'My father died when I was small. My mother was and still is very beautiful and very remote. When I was seven I went away to school and, to be quite honest, I can't recall seeing my mother more than a dozen times in ten years, and then she was always on her way to somewhere else with my two sisters.'

'Oh, how awful,' Anna breathed, imagining him as a small, lonely little boy.

'Don't get me wrong,' he said. 'I'm not fishing for sympathy, far from it. I wasn't unhappy as a child. I learned to be self-sufficient sooner than most, but that isn't a bad thing. It's just that sometimes I get this feeling of nostalgia for what might have been had I been born into any other family but my own.' He smiled. 'But that's enough soul-searching for one day. Let's go and have a look at the river.'

Anna would always remember that afternoon, how the brightness of the sunlight made the rippling surface of the water seem like splintered glass, and how cool it was beneath the willows, the air filled with the fragrance of damp grass and honeysuckle.

They walked along the river bank watching swallows swoop across the water uttering their sharp little cries. A soft breeze riffled the tops of the trees, and they heard a cuckoo calling from the woods around Crossthwaite Manor.

It seemed natural and right that Matt should hold her hand as they walked, and that they should pause at the ancient stone bridge where the mill stream joined the main flow of the river.

'I love this place,' said Anna softly.

Looking back they could see the mill nestled among the trees, while behind them rose Crossthwaite Moor, a high cliff of grey rock covered with gorse and bracken and short harsh grass, where sturdy moorland sheep grazed, apparently indifferent to the tough conditions.

She and Matt leaned over the parapet of the bridge and looked down into the water.

'You're looking very beautiful today,' he said casually.

She was suddenly robbed of breath, unable to tear her eyes from his long brown hands resting against the lichen-covered stones. She noticed neatly clipped fingernails, and the dark hair on his wrists contrasting with the soft pale silk of his shirt cuffs...

Her heart slammed painfully and it felt as though her insides were dissolving in the languid warmth that spread through her, touching each part of her with sharp, tingling anticipation.

She swallowed nervously. 'Thank you.'

His eyes moved over her and her skin quivered, sensitised, aware. 'That dress is the same blue as your eyes. I don't suppose you wore it for me?'

She shook her head, breathless. 'No, not especially.'

Without taking his eyes from hers he said, 'I thought not.'

He reached out and touched her cheek gently, and Anna shivered, feeling as though the whole world suddenly centred on this quiet place, hanging, poised, waiting.

'Anna,' he whispered. He held her face between his hands and she closed her eyes, feeling his breath warm on her skin, unconsciously reaching up to meet his kiss.

His mouth brushed against hers, softly at first, and she felt the feather-light touch of his tongue trace the outline of her lips. She trembled, her legs suddenly weak, and clutched at his shoulders, drawing strength from his strength.

'Sweet little Anna,' he murmured, and she sighed as his arms slid around her, moulding her gently to the hard length of his body, holding her so close she could feel his heartbeats against her breast.

His kiss deepened, his mouth caressing, tantalising, parting her lips, tasting, savouring until she was drowning in a sea of pleasurable sensation. He lifted his head, but kept her inside the circle of his arms. She arched against him; the feel of him was infinitely exciting and she wanted more.

He smiled, his dark grey eyes warm and lazily sensuous. 'Do you believe in love at first sight?'

She laughed throatily. 'That only happens in books, doesn't it? All that stuff about glances across crowded rooms.'

He shook his head and moved away from her. 'Maybe . . . maybe not.' He leaned against the stone wall and slanted a look at her from beneath his brows. 'What would you say if I told you I think I'm in love with you?'

Anna's heart lurched and she caught herself just in time. He was joking of course, and, as long as she remembered that, she could join in his game. 'You don't even know me. How can you fall in love with someone you don't know?'

'What does knowing have to do with anything? I know what I feel, here inside.' He touched his chest, smiling ruefully. 'I feel as if somebody hit me over the head with a hammer. I look into those big blue eyes and feel as if I'm drowning. Is that falling in love? I never felt this way before, so I don't know for sure.'

'I think you must be crazy, but I like it—tell me more.'

He shook his head again. 'You're right, I am crazy. I don't even like little girls with soft curly hair and blue eyes...' He reached for her again, kissing her nose, her cheeks, her eyelids. Then, his hands firmly gripping her upper arms, he put her away from him with a heavy sigh. 'Come on, we'd better get back or you'll be late for your date with friend Doug.'

He held her hand as they walked back along the river bank and Anna was feeling more than slightly bemused by what had just happened between them. She couldn't allow herself to take him seriously when he said he loved her; her own common sense kept telling her such a thing wasn't possible, though she wished with all her heart that it was true.

Matt left as soon as they got back to the mill. Anna saw him to the door and he held her hands tightly.

'Thanks for today,' he said. 'I'm leaving for Kuwait the day after tomorrow and it'll help to have you—and this place—to think about while I'm away.'

Anna tried not to let her disappointment show in her face. After all, what did she expect? He was a stranger just passing through her life, and the fact that he could talk so casually about flying halfway across the world only emphasised the massive gulf between their two life-styles. It was just as well he was going before she allowed herself to become too fond of him...

She smiled and said, 'It's been nice... have a good trip,' realising as she spoke how trite she sounded.

'Oh, sure I will.' He laughed grimly. 'I'll have a real fun time grubbing about in the desert, where it's over a hundred in the shade, listening to a bunch of dumb bastards explain why they spent several million dollars sinking a borehole half a mile away from where I told them to put it.'

'It's not that bad, surely.'

'It is when it's the last place on earth you want to be.'
He grinned at her, and gently touched his lips to her
fingers. 'But I'll be back, in about six weeks. I'll phone
you, OK?'

'OK,' she agreed, not believing for one moment that
he would, but it was nice to dream...

It was raining. Anna locked the green-painted front door
behind her and posted her key through the letterbox,
then, turning abruptly, climbed quickly into the taxi
without looking back.

The rain continued all evening as the taxi sped north-
wards, a fitting background for her mood as she stared
out at the wet green countryside.

She wished there was some way she could switch off
her mind, but the memories went on relentlessly. How
stupid to imagine that running away would help when
Matt was with her every second, mocking her efforts to
escape.

She wondered what he had told his mother. The
thought of Estelle knowing what had happened made
her cringe. Matt's mother hadn't wanted them to marry
in the first place, she had urged them to wait, to get to
know one another better before thinking of marriage,
probably because she was hoping their relationship would
fizzle out eventually. After all, they had so little in
common.

But how long did it take to fall in love, to know that
a particular man was the one above all others to take
your heart and touch your soul with magic?

The rain had stopped by the time she arrived in
Crossthwaite. The sun was setting and in its golden light
a million droplets sparkled like jewels and the air smelled
fresh, of grass and flowers and damp earth.

Anna paused by the garden gate just as a blackbird began its sweet, clear song, piercing the evening stillness with notes of pure liquid sound, almost like a celebration of the joy of living.

She pushed the gate wide and walked along the brick path which led around the side of the house. The garden was a riot of summer flowers: old-fashioned marigolds, nasturtiums and hollyhocks, pale pink tea-roses and honeysuckle. Anna could see where her gran had been weeding, and her gardening gloves and trowel lay on the floor of the porch.

It felt so good to be home.

'Anna, there you are!' Kate cried, hugging her tightly. She held her away, gazing critically into her face. 'You look like hell,' she said bluntly. 'What's happened?'

They went into the bright little kitchen. 'Sit down before you fall down,' Kate ordered. 'I've made soup and salad for supper.'

Anna felt weak tears threatening. She blinked them back. 'I'm not really hungry...'

'Rubbish. That's probably half your trouble. You look starved!'

Kate fussed around her, putting plates and cutlery on the scrubbed pine table, then poured her a mug of hot strong tea. 'Here, get that down you for a start while I put the soup on.'

Anna sipped the tea, feeling the protectiveness of Kate's love warming her as she breathed in the familiar, comforting atmosphere of the house.

Her gran looked the same as always. Though her curly hair was a little greyer these days, her blue eyes were as bright, her movements as brisk as they had ever been. She was wearing her baggy corduroy working trousers, and a navy blue artist's smock. Kate never bothered much about clothes, though Anna knew she had several very smart outfits which she produced when the occasion demanded.

Webster, reclining on the top of the fridge, opened one eye to inspect Anna indifferently, then went back to sleep.

She laughed. 'That cat doesn't change, does he? You'd think he'd at least come and say hello.'

'He's getting old, love.' Kate looked at her, her head on one side. 'Are you going to tell me what's been happening? I had Matt on the phone from New York just after you rang this afternoon. He sounded as if he was on a very short fuse. What have you been doing to the poor boy?'

'I've left him,' Anna said flatly.

Kate's eyes widened in astonishment. 'You've what? Good grief, whatever for?'

Anna rose to her feet, twisting her hands together nervously as she went to stare through the window at the cobbled yard behind the house. 'I left him because he was unfaithful to me,' she said softly, facing her grandmother with tragic eyes.

'Are you sure, love? Do you know who...?'

Anna nodded bitterly. 'Oh, yes, I'm sure. It's his cousin, Sarah.'

'Has he admitted it?'

'No, but——'

'How did you find out?'

'An anonymous phone call, would you believe? It was about five months ago, just after...' She broke off, then, taking a deep, uneven breath, continued, 'Matt was away, on a trip to West Germany, and a woman calling herself a friend rang and said I should ask my husband the truth about his relationship with Sarah Barratt.' She shrugged. 'It was classic. I put a call through to the hotel where he'd said he was staying in Munich, and they told me he wasn't there, and had never even registered.'

'But that still doesn't prove he was with Sarah, does it?' Kate said reasonably.

'No, but as I said, he didn't deny it either. He wasn't even sorry and resented the fact that I'd questioned him at all, his attitude being that his extramarital activities were none of my damned business.'

'But if all this happened five months ago, why didn't you leave then?'

'I don't know. I felt terribly hurt, but I still wanted to give him the benefit of the doubt. I felt that if he'd apologised, made some kind of excuse and promised it wouldn't happen again, I could have forgiven him. It was clutching at straws, I suppose.' She sighed heavily. 'Then we went to this party in New York the other night, and I saw him kissing Sarah... I just can't take any more, Gran!'

'Do you think you're over-reacting, Anna?' Kate asked gently. 'After all, things have been pretty fraught for you since the baby...'

Anna shook her head impatiently. 'This has nothing to do with the baby.' She clenched her fists. 'I love... loved Matt, and I thought he loved me too... I don't know what happened to us. It seems as though we've been papering over the cracks in our marriage for ages, and now they've become like bottomless chasms, and we're standing on either side, not even facing one another any more.' She shook her head wearily. 'I'm so tired of it all. I just want some peace.'

Kate put her arms around Anna and gently stroked her hair. The girl seemed terribly thin, her blue eyes clouded with pain and exhaustion.

'Listen, love, you get yourself up to bed right now. I'll bring you some supper on a tray and then you can get a good night's sleep. We'll have another talk about all this in the morning and decide what to do. All right?'

Anna nodded. At that moment the thought of bed in her own room, with her old familiar childhood things about her, seemed infinitely welcoming.

Yet after her gran had gone, taking the barely touched supper tray back to the kitchen, Anna found it impossible to drop off to sleep despite her exhaustion.

She wondered what Matt was likely to do when he found her gone. Would he follow her to Crossthwaite? She thought not—he had too much pride for that. Once he realised she meant what she said, that would be it, finished.

But in that case, she argued, why come back to England at all? Common sense told her that, after flying all the way home from New York, he was bound to come the last few miles to Crossthwaite, and it was sheer lunacy to imagine herself out of his reach at the mill.

Matthew let himself into the cottage, swearing as he tripped over a large cardboard box standing in the middle of the tiny hall.

'What the devil's this?' he muttered, lifting the flaps. He saw one of Anna's Neil Diamond LPs on the top and knew then exactly what it was. Further investigation showed her clothes gone from her half of their huge wardrobe, her embroidery frame missing from its usual place by the sitting-room window.

He clenched his fists, and, resisting with extreme difficulty the serious urge to smash something, he reached for the phone.

Kate answered. 'Will you put Anna on, Kate, please?' he demanded tersely.

'I don't know if she'll speak to you, Matt, but I'll go and ask her. She's in the garden so you'll have to hang on a minute.'

Kate's voice was cool, and Matt experienced a twinge of regret. He was very fond of Anna's gran.

Several minutes passed, during which he became gradually more impatient and was about to slam the receiver down when he heard Anna's voice on the other end of the line.

'What do you want?' she asked quietly.

Anger wiped all thoughts of tact and diplomacy from his mind. 'I told you to stay put, didn't I?' he replied savagely.

Again that quiet, self-possessed little voice, putting him firmly in his place as she said, 'Where are you now?'

'At the cottage. I just got back. I'm tired and dirty and hungry, and why the hell aren't you here?'

'You don't need me, Matt, you're more than capable of looking after yourself. As for why I didn't hang around at the cottage waiting for you, well, I didn't see any point.'

'You're determined to see this through to the bitter end?' His voice was scornful, disbelieving.

'I'm not coming back, if that's what you mean.'

There was a pause before he said, 'Look, we have to talk. You can't just walk out on me like this.'

'I already did.'

He pushed his fingers through his hair distractedly. 'It's our marriage, for heaven's sake. Doesn't that mean anything to you?'

'About as much as it means to you!' she snapped, adding furiously, 'Look, don't try your subtle blackmail on me, Matt! Don't force your double standards down my throat, and, most of all, don't try and make me take responsibility for your mistakes!'

'All right,' he said, forcing himself to be patient with her. 'All right, I'm sorry, but we've still got to talk about it.'

'I don't want to talk about it. There is nothing to talk about, can't you understand that?'

He sighed wearily. 'Always dodging the issue, aren't you, Anna? Don't you have the guts to stand up and fight?'

'You and I have done enough fighting. I just want some peace, so please leave me alone.'

Unable to restrain himself, Matt swore violently, and heard a click as she put the phone down on him.

He stared at the empty chair where Anna used to sit, a folder filled with old embroidery designs that she'd forgotten to pack, the little framed water-colour she'd bought him for his last birthday, and felt his guts twist inside him as the almost hopeless desperation he had been keeping at bay for the past six months threatened to overwhelm him. Until now, work had been his salvation, enabling him to switch off, to concentrate his thoughts for a few hours each day at least on something other than Anna and the wall of silence between them.

He poured himself a drink, realising momentarily that it was still only nine-thirty in the morning. But what the hell, he thought, draining the glass with a grimace.

The cuffs on his shirt were grubby and he peeled it off with a feeling of disgust. Upstairs he showered quickly, and dressed again in a fresh set of clothes, deliberately not looking at the empty half of the wardrobe. Then, without stopping to eat, he went back out to his car.

CHAPTER FOUR

ANNA leaned against the wall, trembling, emotionally drained, and Kate touched her arm gently.

'All right?'

She nodded, smiling weakly. 'I put the phone down on him.'

'Is he coming here?'

'He didn't say, but he's bound to. He says we have to talk.'

'I agree with him there. You do have to talk, and get something worked out between you, though it's better to do it here, on neutral ground, as it were.' Kate reached behind the kitchen door for her pottery overall. 'Now, I must get some work done. Why don't you pop down to the village and see Lucy at the shop? And while you're there you'd better pick up a loaf and some eggs, and some bacon too if Matt's coming. You know what an appetite he has.'

'Gran,' Anna protested, laughing in spite of herself, 'if Matt comes, he's certainly not getting the fatted-calf treatment. Let him feed elsewhere.'

'Serious talking is better done across the dinner table. It gives you something to do with your hands,' said Kate firmly.

Anna walked the half-mile to Crossthwaite village. The narrow road ran between drystone walls, beyond which were fields of rough pasture where sheep and cattle grazed. She breathed deeply, enjoying the freshness of the country after the bustle and fumes of London.

She and Matt had been obliged to make the city their base, but she had never really felt at ease there. There was something so indifferent about the city; she had the feeling that, had she died right there on the pavement, people would have just stepped over her and carried on with their lives.

Crossthwaite, in the heart of the Yorkshire Dales, consisted of a single meandering street of stone-built cottages running alongside the river, with a picturesque humpbacked bridge and an ancient church. It had long ago geared itself to the demands of tourism, with two cafés, three antique shops, as well as Anna's and Lucy's gift shop.

She opened the door and stepped inside, breathing in the familiar scents of pot-pourri and new leather. Wind-bells tinkled softly in the draught from the open door, and Lucy glanced up from serving a customer, her red hair gleaming like a beacon, her face split by a wide grin as she called, 'Just the person I wanted to see,' at the top of her voice down the length of the shop, making several browsing tourists turn and stare.

Anna nodded politely at them and made her way past the shelves and baskets overflowing with an assortment of craftware, everything from her gran's Mill Pottery to herb pillows, leatherwork and handmade jewellery, to framed water-colours by local artists and her own embroideries.

'I thought you were in the States. I was going to phone you at the weekend,' said Lucy breathlessly. 'Is Matt with you?'

'Not at the moment. I am capable of independent movement, you know.'

Lucy pursed her lips. 'If that gorgeous hunk belonged to me I wouldn't let him out of my sight.' She broke off to serve her customers, and when they'd gone said, 'Come into the back and we'll have coffee and a chat.'

Lucy made instant coffee and produced a box of chocolate biscuits from a cupboard. 'Now, tell me all your news. How was New York?' she said, and settling herself comfortably on a stool looked carefully at Anna's face. 'You seem a bit strung up. Is everything all right—between you and Matt, I mean?'

Anna sighed. 'You might as well know now as later—I've left him.'

'Oh . . . oh, I am sorry. Do you want to talk about it?'

'Not right now, Lucy. It's . . . well, a bit raw at the moment.'

'I understand.' Lucy helped herself to a biscuit and chewed thoughtfully for a while. Then she said, 'I would never have believed it. You two seemed so right for one another.'

'Which just goes to show how wrong you can be, doesn't it?' Anna said, the lightness in her tone belying the pain in her blue eyes.

'Things might work out, you know,' Lucy said hopefully. 'And, in the meantime, I'm always here if you need an ear. A confidential ear,' she added.

'Yes, I know, and . . . thanks.' Anna smiled. 'What about you and Doug, have you decided on a wedding date yet?'

Lucy shrugged, her mouth turned down as she said, 'You must be joking. I think the only way I'll get Doug to the altar is under hypnosis, which doesn't do a great deal for my ego. I sometimes wonder if I should give him up as a lost cause and try for someone a little more willing.' She smiled ruefully. 'The trouble is, I love the stupid idiot.'

The two girls discussed the shop in general until the arrival of another group of customers put an end to their conversation, and Anna was never more relieved that she had ignored Matt's advice to sell out her share in Treasures after they were married. It meant she would be able to earn her own living and not be a burden to her gran, nor would she be obliged to take anything from Matt. Right now her own financial independence was an important bulwark to her battered pride.

She left the shop deep in thought, then paused when a voice called her name, 'Hey, Anna, wait!' and, turning, her face relaxed into a smile as she saw Doug Whitacker hurrying towards her.

'I thought it was you,' he said breathlessly. 'When did you get back? Kate didn't say you were coming.'

'No, it was a spur-of-the-moment thing. I got back last night,' she told him.

'Is your husband with you?'

It was odd, but Doug and Matt had never like one another, Anna realised now. To Doug, Matt was merely Anna's husband, while Matt referred to Doug as 'your friend, what's-his-name', and even Doug's subsequent engagement to Lucy hadn't changed his attitude.

'Matt's in London,' she said and saw the satisfaction in Doug's face. She'd known him forever and was well aware that her gran and his mother had hoped they'd marry eventually.

She might even have married Doug if Matt hadn't come on the scene. She was fond of him, in a peaceful, uncomplicated kind of way, though he had never indicated anything more than brotherly affection for her.

But he hadn't married either and she found herself wondering why. He was nice to look at, with brown hair and hazel eyes, and he had a good steady job as headmaster of the village primary school. He'd make a perfect husband for any girl.

But not me, she realised, thinking it strange how one man could be a friend, while another had that magic something that could fill her heart and satisfy her soul.

'Will you be staying long this time?' Doug asked.

'For the time being, yes.'

'Look, come and have coffee with me. I have half an hour to spare.'

The last thing Anna wanted was to sit in a café with Doug and play the 'Do you remember?' game. They had been very close once, but that was light years ago. She was a different person now from the carefree girl he had taken to discos and school fund-raising functions. She recognised the change in herself and felt constrained by it, and shaking her head said, 'Another time, Doug. I just had coffee with Lucy at the shop, now I must get back or Gran will think I'm lost.'

'Can I give you a lift to the mill, then?'

He looked so eager, and she was feeling a little tired, so she agreed to let him drive her home.

His car was a sensible family hatchback, not in the least sporty, like Matt's Jaguar XJS. He held the door for her and made sure she was safely belted in before starting the engine.

Doug cleared his throat, then said hesitantly, 'I never got a chance to tell you how sorry I was—we were— about... well, you know...'

'The baby? Yes, I know. I got your card... It was good to know people, friends were thinking of us.'

'Have you been happy, Anna? I mean apart from what happened with your baby.'

The question surprised her. 'Let's just say I got what I deserved,' she replied flippantly, not realising her bright smile did nothing to dispel the bleakness in her eyes.

'You should have married me, you know,' he said suddenly. 'I was just getting up the courage to ask you when that city slicker whisked you away from under my nose.' He laughed and the sound was bitter. 'I remember thinking at the time, there you go, Doug Whitacker, pipped at the post again.'

She stared at him. 'I never knew... Oh, Doug, I don't know what to say...'

He slanted a look at her. 'Don't say anything. I'm just feeling sorry for myself, that's all. Forget I spoke.'

Anna felt extremely uncomfortable, and guilty, and wished profoundly that he had kept his mouth shut. She couldn't deal with this right now, and, after all, she was sure he had never given her any indication that he was working up to a proposal. They had enjoyed one another's company as friends, never as lovers.

'That's OK,' she said. 'I'm sorry if I hurt you, but I never thought... Oh, hell, I feel so guilty!'

'Look, don't. It was my own fault for not speaking out when I had the chance. I'm a coward, that's all there is to it.' He sighed heavily. 'Anyway, it was probably for the best, and I have Lucy...'

Anna glanced at him and he smiled his familiar lopsided smile. Would she have been safer with Doug? she wondered. Perhaps it was a mistake to expect too much. Maybe it would have been better to choose steady affection rather than blazing passion which burned itself out all too soon, leaving nothing but dead ashes in its wake.

She didn't understand. She only knew that Matt had had the power to reach and touch every part of her with magic, making her feel as though the time before he came into her life had counted for nothing.

She covered Doug's hand with her own. 'Yes, you do have Lucy, and she loves you very much.'

They passed the rest of the journey in an awkward silence. 'Are you coming in to say hello to Gran?' Anna asked when he stopped the car outside the mill, then felt profound relief when he shook his head.

'I'd better not. I promised to take Mother shopping in town and she gets a bit tight-lipped if I'm late.'

'Thanks for the lift,' she said. 'See you?'

He smiled. 'I expect so. I'm usually around.'

Kate was in the kitchen, chopping vegetables for a casserole. 'Matt phoned again while you were out,' she remarked casually.

'He doesn't give up, does he?' Anna said. 'What did he want this time?'

'Just to tell us he'll be arriving mid-afternoon.'

Anna felt a surge of panic. 'Oh, lord, why the hell can't he leave me alone? I don't want to even see him, let alone have to talk to him right now!'

Kate looked at her. 'You're going to have to deal with this, Anna, and it might as well be now as later. This kind of thing doesn't improve with keeping, you know. Now, make us a cup of tea and calm down.'

Anna took her tea outside. The mill yard basked silently in the warm sun and she could see Webster sprawled flat out in his usual place on top of the wall.

'It's all right for you, cat,' she muttered, thinking that he had a lot to answer for.

Leaving her empty cup on the wall, she walked down to the river, trying to calm her shattered nerves. After all, she was the injured party; there was no need for her to be on the defensive, or to feel in the least guilty.

She sat on the river bank idly tossing pebbles into the water as she tried to keep her anger alive. But all she could think of was Matt's face when they made love, dark and savage with passion. His laughter when she said something that amused him. The way he used to reach out and touch her when she passed his chair. His tenderness, his love.

She lay back in the warm grass on the river bank and folded her hands behind her head, letting her thoughts drift aimlessly backwards...

Matt hadn't phoned when he came back from Kuwait. Instead he had turned up at the mill without warning, bringing chocolates for Kate, a little grey clockwork mouse for Webster, and a huge bouquet of yellow roses for Anna.

Anna had opened the door, and just stood there staring at him like a fool.

He smiled. 'Aren't you going to ask me in?'

'Oh...yes, of course.' She held the door wide. He had to turn sideways to get the bouquet through the opening and he dumped it into her arms with a laugh.

'Here, you'd better have these and put them in water before they wilt.'

She clutched the flowers to her, breathing in their delicate scent. 'Are these for me?'

'Who else? I hope you like roses. The woman in the flower shop seemed to think they were the thing to buy.'

She laughed. 'Well, she would, wouldn't she? Thank you so much, they're beautiful.'

He leaned down and kissed her mouth lightly. 'Glad you like them.'

He stayed for dinner and afterwards they went for a walk along the river bank as far as the bridge. He put his arm around her and she knew she had never been as happy as she was that night.

'I missed you,' he said when they stopped on the bridge. 'Can you believe that?'

'I don't know,' she replied, tensely aware of him beside her. He held her close to his side and she could feel his warmth through the thin cotton of her dress. 'It was lovely of you to bring the flowers and things, but we don't really know one another, do we?' She was trying to be sensible, to rationalise her feelings.

He shrugged. 'I could be with you for a year and know no more about you than I do right now.'

'That's a depressing thought.'

'It depends on your point of view, Anna, my love.' He turned to look at her, his hands resting lightly on her shoulders, his eyes moving over her face as if to learn her features one by one and engrave them on his memory for all time.

'I feel as if I've known you all my life,' he said softly. His hand touched her cheek, fingers caressing. 'I could fill a book with the things I know about you and it still wouldn't be enough.'

She laughed nervously, feeling her heart slamming against her ribs. 'That's crazy.' It was crazy, yet she understood exactly. It was as if she had been waiting for him all her life, as if she had finally discovered where she wanted to belong, for always.

Shyly, she reached out to touch his face; he grasped her wrist and pressed a kiss to her madly fluttering pulse, then drew her into his arms.

'Anna, I love you,' he said, almost wonderingly.

And she had believed him, and gone on believing and trusting, and loving. And it had seemed so natural and right when he drew her down into the long fragrant grass beneath the willows...

But that was before, Anna told herself firmly, thrusting away the memory of that time, the first time they had made love in the cool green shadows by the river in what had seemed like a perfect mating of hearts and bodies, making them one, united for all time. Though it had been an illusion, she realised now, because in the end there had been nothing; his love had changed, to boredom, to irritation and finally to indifference.

She suddenly became aware of a sound coming from the direction of the river: a frightened howling, a cat in distress.

Webster, she thought, jumping to her feet. Webster's in the river! Then she saw something floating, a sack caught up in a clump of reeds, and as she watched it moved and she heard again the anguished howls.

'Oh, no,' she whispered, appalled, furiously angry, and, without thinking about her shoes, waded into the river and reached for the sack.

The water soaked through her jeans, feeling shockingly chilly against her legs, and her feet sank into the muddy bottom. She grabbed the sack and brought it quickly to the bank, losing one of her shoes in the process.

'There you are, puss,' she said softly. 'We'll soon have you out.' She knelt, trying to calm the animal as she pulled at the string around the top of the sack. She didn't hear the car coming down the lane, she didn't hear anything above the cat's frantic screams until an incredulous voice demanded,

'What the devil are you up to now?'

She glanced up, pushing at her hair with a filthy hand as she stared at Matt, shock making her numb, speechless, while her heart began its slow, heavy pounding in her breast.

She licked her lips and tasted mud. Under her hands the sack continued to heave and Matt glanced down at it, an amused smile curving his mouth.

'I know I'll probably regret asking, but just what are you doing with that?'

'It was in the river. I fished it out but I can't undo the string. Help me, please.' The words came out in a rush, breathlessly.

'Allow me.' He took a small penknife from his pocket and neatly severed the wet string around the neck of the sack, then stepped hastily back to a safe distance as Anna unwrapped a small, bedraggled and enraged tabby cat.

'Oh, you poor little thing.' She reached out to touch it and quick as a flash a razor-tipped paw lashed at her, inflicting a vicious scratch across her knuckles. 'Ouch! There's ingratitude!' she cried as the cat bounded on to the wall and sat twitching its tail.

'Retaliation is only to be expected, Anna,' said Matt calmly. 'I doubt it'll have much trust for people after such a nasty experience. Here, let me have a look at that scratch.'

She rubbed the blood away on her dirty T-shirt. 'It's nothing.'

'For heaven's sake, don't do that. You've probably got a billion germs in there already.'

'Don't fuss, I expect Gran will have some antiseptic in the house.'

'Just as well,' said Matt wearily. He retreated a step, grimacing. 'Phew, you stink to high heaven—a bath might be a good idea. And where's your other shoe?'

'In the river.' Anna glared at him. She was well aware she needed a bath, but it didn't help to have him say so.

Matt, as usual, was immaculately dressed, in well-fitting brown trousers and a silk shirt, making her feel even more scruffy by comparison.

She hesitated, unsure what to do about the cat, which was busily grooming itself on top of the wall, with an occasional suspicious glance in their direction.

Matt noticed her indecision and laughed. 'Don't worry about him, he's well able to take care of himself. Which is more than I can say for you.'

His disparaging tone got her back up immediately. 'And just what do you mean by that?'

The dark grey eyes spoke volumes as they flicked over her. 'Well, just look at yourself.'

'Thanks!' She turned and stalked back to the house, trying for aloof dignity, despite her one bare foot.

Nothing ever went as she planned, she thought resentfully. She had planned to be cool and self-possessed, to remain calm while they had a civilised discussion about their future. Instead he had arrived early, to find her grovelling in the mud.

She left her remaining shoe outside the kitchen door and went across to the sink to clean the mud from her hands, letting warm water run over the scratch, which stung quite painfully. Matt leaned against the doorframe, watching her, an enigmatic little smile tugging his lips. Anna avoided looking at him. His mere presence turned her legs to jelly and her only refuge was in anger.

'You're early,' she snapped. 'Gran said you wouldn't be here till later.'

He shrugged. 'I couldn't wait to be with you, darling.'

'Don't you darling me!' She slammed cupboard doors in her search for the first-aid box. 'And how did you manage to drive all the way from London in such a short time?'

'I didn't, of course. There's a car out there, not a jet. I was already at junction twenty-one and phoned from the motorway services.'

'A typically sneaky move on your part,' Anna said belligerently. She found the box beside the cake tin in the larder. Inside, apart from the antiseptic, was a varied selection of potions for cat ailments, which showed quite clearly where Kate's priorities lay as far as medical matters were concerned.

Anna glared at Matt as she dabbed antiseptic lotion on her hand. 'Why have you come here, anyway? I told you I want you to leave me alone.'

He shrugged. 'I don't give much of a damn what you want.' And, advancing into the kitchen, he hooked a chair from beneath the table and straddled it, leaning his arms on the back. 'You surely didn't imagine I'd let you go, just like that?'

'You don't have any choice, do you? Besides, I can't believe you want to continue this...this farce any more than I.'

'If by farce you mean our marriage, if it ends it will be on my terms, not yours,' he said calmly.

'Oh, really? Can't you bear the thought of the world knowing I walked out on you? Don't worry, I'm not about to tell anyone.'

'Don't push me, Anna.' His voice was soft with menace, his slate-dark glance flicked over her and she shivered. Then he smiled. 'Isn't it customary to offer guests a drink or something?'

'You are hardly a guest!' she retorted.

He sighed. 'OK, but I've driven a long way, I'm tired and I'd like some coffee.'

'So, am I your waitress? If you want coffee, or anything else for that matter, you can get it yourself. I'm going up for a bath!'

'Thanks,' he said drily, 'your hospitality overwhelms me.'

'Oh, go to hell!' she muttered, feeling a small twinge of guilt. He did look tired, as well he might after all the travelling he'd done in the past twenty-four hours.

But nobody had asked him to do it, had they? she thought. For whatever reason, it had been his own idea to come after her.

She locked the bathroom door, and, dropping her muddy clothes on to the floor, looked at herself in the old full-length mirror. Its surface was misty with age and gave her pale skin a golden bloom which was quite flattering.

Unbidden into her mind came the memory of how Matt's hands had felt on her body. She trembled and, feeling a familiar aching warmth inside, turned away from her reflection. It did no good to remember. Those memories made her weak. Better instead to think of Matt with Sarah and keep her anger alive.

She stayed in the bath a long time, her mind empty of thought, floating in the silky warmth, her body relaxed and drowsy. Until she heard Matt at the door.

'Anna, are you all right?'

She didn't answer him. What was he doing here anyway? He'd always said he'd never follow her if she left him, so why was he here?

'Anna, answer me before I break this bloody door down!'

'Go away!' she yelled back.

'Come out of there.' He was speaking normally now. 'Kate's cooked dinner and the least you can do is come down and eat it.'

'I don't want any dinner.'

'You'll do as you're told!'

'Get lost!'

At once she heard him forcing the door. The lock was old and not equal to the struggle—it gave way after two hefty blows, and Anna sank beneath the water as Matt approached the bath.

'I did warn you,' he said pleasantly.

'Get out of here, you . . . you vandal!' She tried, unsuccessfully, to cover herself with her face-cloth and he laughed at her.

'Modesty, darling? You do surprise me.' And reaching down he pulled the plug, then handed her a towel. 'Come on out, or are you going to vanish down the plug-hole with the water?'

Anna grabbed the towel and wrapped it around herself. 'You bastard!'

He grinned. 'If you say so. Now, you have five minutes to get dressed so I suggest you stop behaving like a spoilt child and get a move on.'

Anna stood in the empty bath, naked, trembling, vulnerable. 'I hate you!' she muttered as he strode from the bathroom, though not quite loud enough for him to hear.

Her teeth chattered with sudden cold and she rubbed herself dry quickly. Then, pulling on the first thing that came to hand when she opened her wardrobe, a black cotton T-shirt dress that Matt had always disliked, she went back downstairs with her damp hair wrapped in a towel.

Matt had made coffee and handed her a mug across the table. 'Sit down and I'll dry your hair,' he said, reaching for the towel.

'There's no need, I can do it myself, thank you.' She was still shivering and couldn't look at him, and her arms felt heavy when she lifted her hands to her hair.

'Don't be awkward,' Matt said softly. He pushed her on to a stool and, taking the towel, began to rub vigorously at her short curls.

Knowing when she was beaten, she let him do it without argument, closing her eyes against sudden tears as she felt his familiar touch, his warmth against her back.

Once her hair was dry he took the brush and eased away the tangles, smoothing the soft baby curls back from her face. Then his hand slowed, stroking sensuously along her neck, and she stiffened, feeling a quiver of awareness like a shock through her body. His thighs were hard against her back and her blood pounded.

His fingers encircled her slender throat and caressed the fragile collarbones, before moving to excite the sensitive hollows beneath her ears. He cupped her chin between his palms and tipped her head back, exposing the pale column of her neck.

She stared up at him; his eyes were dark and the light from the window threw the strong contours of his face into sharp relief, giving him an almost satanic look as he slid his hands down to her breasts, pressing her to his thighs, moving the lean strength of his hips against her shoulderblades.

'Anna,' he said softly, smiling. 'Kiss me...'

She licked her lips; they felt soft, and parted eagerly for his kiss. For vital seconds she forgot everything between them as all her thoughts and emotions became concentrated on her need to be in his arms. She twisted on the stool and reached for him, her hands on his shoulders drawing him down to her waiting mouth...

The clock on the wall chimed the half-hour, the sound loud in the stillness, shattering the moment, leaving her appalled by her own weakness.

Matt drew away from her at once, a shutter of indifference quenching the passion in his eyes as he glanced at the clock. 'Perhaps it's just as well...' he said lightly. 'Hardly the best moment to choose with Kate likely to walk in on us at any moment.' He chuckled. 'Not to worry, there's plenty of time.'

Gathering her scattered wits, Anna glared at him. 'You've got a nerve! And what do you mean, there's plenty of time?'

'I have six weeks' leave, remember.' He eyed the black dress with distaste. 'Do you have to wear that thing? It makes you look sick.'

Ignoring his remark, Anna pushed at her hair with fingers that trembled. 'You're planning to spend your leave here?'

'Where else?' he replied. 'You're my wife. It's the usual thing for a man to spend his time off with his wife.'

'Or his girlfriend,' she pointed out acidly.

'Granted, but on this particular occasion I chose you, you lucky girl,' he leered, making a joke of it.

Anna didn't see the funny side. 'You can't stay here!'

'Why not? Who's to object—not Kate, surely? And besides, as I said before, you ain't gonna get away that easy.'

Anna turned away in exasperation. She didn't like Matt in this mood, nastily amusing, with a hard expression in his grey eyes, and decided to ignore him.

Kate came in the door carrying Webster. 'Hello, Matt, I thought I heard your car. You made good time, didn't you, dear?' She put Webster down and he jumped up to his usual place on top of the fridge. 'We seem to have acquired a freeloader,' she told them, laughing. 'There's a scruffy-looking tabby out there helping himself to Webster's dinner. I brought the poor old fellow inside because I think he'd probably come off worse in a scrap.'

'I fished him out of the river, Gran,' Anna said indignantly. 'Someone had tried to drown him in a sack.'

'Good grief, you wouldn't believe people could do such a thing, and in a little place like this. I sometimes wonder what the world's coming to, I really do.' She sighed. 'Well, at least the poor thing's getting a good dinner after his ordeal. And, talking of dinner, has anyone looked at the casserole?'

'I have,' said Matt. 'It seems to be OK, and certainly smells fantastic.'

Kate smiled. 'I'll just wash my hands, then we'll eat.'

CHAPTER FIVE

KATE and Matt chatted companionably throughout the meal, just as though everything were normal. Anna felt odd, removed, almost as if she were standing outside herself watching the three of them.

How polite and civilised we all are, she thought, not in the least surprised when Kate announced her intention of having an early night.

When she had gone, leaving them at opposite ends of the sitting-room like strangers, Matt leaned back in his chair, looking at Anna from beneath his brows, until she felt herself squirm like a butterfly on a pin.

'Do I have a smut on my nose?' she asked brightly.

He laughed. 'No, your little nose is as smut-free and delectable as always.'

She eyed him dangerously. 'Look, don't start that. I don't want any of your flippant remarks and personal comments. You came here to talk to me, so talk, but don't expect me to listen to what you have to say.'

'That's rather a negative attitude, isn't it, darling? How can we hope to solve our problems if you won't negotiate?'

'What do you think this is, a bloody union meeting or something?'

He shrugged. 'It's the same kind of situation.'

'Oh, for heaven's sake!' she said furiously. 'You talk as though you're sitting round the boardroom table discussing business tactics. What about feelings, emotions?'

'You tell me, love. I didn't notice much regard for my feelings when you ran out on me in New York. You made me look a bloody fool.'

'And that's all you care about, isn't it?' she said witheringly. 'I made you look a fool. Well, that's just too bad. Now you know how it feels, don't you?'

Her tone annoyed him, she could tell by the set of his mouth and the hardness in his grey eyes.

'Anna,' he said between clenched teeth, 'it might be a good idea if we could at least pretend to be civilised people. I didn't come here to fight with you. I think you and I have gone way past that stage.'

'I agree. Fighting means there's something left in a relationship, even if it's only animosity. For us to fight is like kicking a corpse!'

'What a charming turn of phrase,' he said wearily.

Anna went to look through the window. It had started to rain and the brick path gleamed wetly. She hoped the little stray cat had found itself somewhere warm to sleep for the night.

'Why did you come here?' she asked quietly.

'I had to see you. Let's face it, you can't just walk out on a relationship leaving a lot of ragged ends. It's untidy to say the least.' He smiled bitterly. 'When I realised you'd gone, I was very angry. I wanted to wring your lovely little neck, though I did manage to calm down about mid-Atlantic. I thought that when I got here you'd have had time to reflect, maybe regret a little, to cool down sufficiently to take rational discussion.'

She turned to face him. 'You think I'm being irrational?'

'Don't you?'

Anna stared at him with dislike. He was so arrogant, so sure of himself. She had never known him to fail at anything he tried, except their marriage, of course, and even that wasn't entirely his fault. She was honest enough with herself in admitting that much at least.

But she hadn't been unfaithful.

She heard Matt sigh heavily. 'I've had to live with your holier than thou attitude and it's been no fun, believe me. Quite frankly, I've had a gutful of martyred glances, tears and sleeping in the spare room.'

She clenched her fists, longing to hit him. 'You are a callous, unfeeling bastard!'

'Because I don't choose to wallow in self-pity like you? Because I refused to allow one tragedy to blight my whole life?' He rose angrily to his feet. 'Daniel was my son too, Anna. I loved him too...' His voice softened. 'I loved him too. But you never stopped to consider that.' He took a deep breath. 'You never cared how I was feeling, did you? You just shut me out and refused to face reality.' He shook his head as she opened her mouth to speak. 'But, as you said, it's too late. All we can do now is pick up the pieces and go our separate ways. That's what you want, isn't it?'

Anna swallowed. Faced with the direct question, she couldn't bring herself to say the words he wanted to hear. 'Do we have to talk about it tonight?'

'We must, my love,' he said, the endearment a hateful contradiction to the bleakness in his eyes. 'We were one, now we are two, and there are things to be settled before this wretched business is done with. Unless, of course, you'd rather leave it all to the lawyers?'

The idea of some impersonal solicitor dissecting the small print of her life with Matt was repugnant to her. Far better, and less painful in the long run, to do as Matt suggested and settle these things between them first.

Her lips felt frozen as she said, 'All right. Go ahead, I'm listening.'

She felt a numbing sense of unreality as he talked, made decisions as to what was to be done with the things they owned. He spoke coolly, with almost clinical detachment, like somebody discussing the weather. She realised he must have given it a great deal of thought to be so matter-of-fact and knew then that their separation would be a welcome solution to him.

But for Anna it was horrible, shocking, a tearing apart of something once real and alive and very precious to her.

'It's up to you,' he was saying. 'All I ask is that we keep it on a civilised footing. I don't want any grubby in-fighting over who gets the washing-machine, if you see what I mean.' He smiled wryly. 'You and I are two people who failed to make a go of our marriage. I don't like failure, Anna, it sticks in my throat...' He rose to his feet. 'I'm going to make some coffee. Want some?'

'What...? Oh, yes, please.' Grateful for something to do, she followed him into the kitchen and found mugs and spoons while he filled the percolator.

This is like a horrible dream, Anna thought. It was like being on the slide when she was a little girl. Once you pushed off from the top you couldn't go back, no matter how the height scared you. You could slow yourself down by putting your hands on the sides, but the end result was just the same.

Her hands trembled, she dropped one of the mugs and it shattered on the tiled floor.

'Hell!' she muttered, and reached for the dustpan. But suddenly her eyes were so full of tears that she couldn't see to sweep up the pieces, and she knelt there, crying hopelessly until Matt took the dustpan from her and drew her into his arms.

'Stop, Anna,' he said gently. 'Please, don't cry.'

She couldn't bear the pity in his voice and tore away from him, rubbing her hands across her eyes as she cried hoarsely, 'Leave me alone, do you hear? Just leave me alone!' and ran from the room.

The next morning was bright, with sunshine making diamonds of the rain that had fallen during the night. Anna woke early after a disturbed sleep which left dark shadows beneath her eyes.

The house was very quiet, but when she went into the bathroom she saw the mirror was steamy, and there was a faint odour of toothpaste and lemon soap, which meant Matt was already up.

In the kitchen the coffee-pot was still hot and the back door stood wide open. Anna poured herself a cup of coffee and sat down facing the door to wait.

She knew Matt had gone for a walk. He was an early riser and often went walking at the crack of dawn in all weathers. When they were first married, he would wake her when he returned from these jaunts, his lips cool when he kissed her, his body smelling of fresh air, his hair sometimes wet with rain. She would hold his coolness in her warm arms and he would want her then. He would undress quickly and come back to their bed to make love...

Anna shifted uncomfortably, feeling weak with sudden hunger for him. If only he'd come through that door now and take her into his arms, if only...

She heard his tuneless whistle as he walked along the garden path, and her pulses began to race. She sat motionless, staring at the open doorway and, suddenly, he filled it: tall, lean-hipped in tight denim jeans and a faded shirt open halfway down to show the dark hair on his chest.

He saw her and paused momentarily, his eyes expressionless as they flicked over her, lingering on her face, her hair.

'Good morning,' he said. 'How are you feeling?'

'Fine, thanks. Did you enjoy your walk?'

'Yes, it's a beautiful morning. I went as far as the manor.'

How polite we are, thought Anna, like strangers instead of two people who have known each other as intimately as is possible between a man and a woman. 'What would you like for breakfast?' she asked.

He grinned. 'I'm famished—it must be all this fresh country air. How about eggs, bacon, the works?'

Her stomach heaved at the thought of fried food, but she managed a smile as she reached into the fridge for the bacon.

'It's a great pity no one ever did anything about the manor,' Matt said. 'A place like that shouldn't go to waste.'

Anna shrugged. 'It'll cost too much to rebuild. That's why the company didn't buy it after all, isn't it?'

Matt nodded. 'In the end the board decided it was more cost-effective to put up a purpose-built research unit.'

He made fresh coffee and toast, and Anna slid his eggs and bacon on to a warm plate.

'Aren't you having any?' he asked.

'I couldn't, not this time of day,' she mumbled.

He frowned. 'You don't eat enough. You'll make yourself ill.'

She stared at him. 'Matt, we have been married for eighteen months and in all that time you have never seen me eat a cooked breakfast,' she said patiently. 'Didn't you notice, for goodness' sake?'

'Of course I noticed. How could I not with your shrinking before my very eyes? Is it some kind of campaign to make me feel guilty?'

'Don't be absurd. Why should I want to make you feel guilty?'

'Lord knows, unless it's all tied up with your over-heated ideas about Sarah and me.'

'Ah, I wondered when you'd get around to mentioning her,' Anna said acidly. 'Dear Sarah. Does she know I've left you?'

'As a matter of fact she does.'

'I'm amazed you aren't with her, then, at the famous Malibu beach house.'

'You've got to be kidding. Malibu is not my idea of somewhere to spend a holiday.'

'Even with darling Sarah?'

'Especially with darling Sarah,' he said grimly. He put down his knife and fork and looked at her across the table. 'Listen, Anna, you've got to understand about Sarah and me...'

'What is there to understand?' she asked, feeling needles of pain slice through her. 'I saw all I needed to see in New York, remember?'

'What you saw in New York was a tipsy kiss at a party and nothing more,' he said dismissively.

'Really?' Anna's voice was loaded with sarcasm. 'Well, I'm sorry I can't be modern and liberated about that kind of thing, but that's the way I am. Old-fashioned, I know, but I happen to believe marriage vows are for keeping.'

Matt sighed heavily. 'OK, but what I want to know is how you feel about forgiveness, because that's part of it too, you know.'

Their eyes met and Anna shook her head. 'I don't know, Matt. You'll have to give me time to think about it.' Trembling, she rose to her feet and went through into the sitting-room.

She pushed back the pale gold curtains and opened the french window on to a small terrace of grey flagstones. The air was fresh with the scent of rainwashed grass, and climbing roses hung heavy wet heads, scattering petals like confetti.

The door opened behind her and Matt came into the room. She didn't need to turn her head to know he was there. She sensed his nearness, heard his soft breath, felt his warmth as he came to stand beside her by the open window.

He reached out to touch her hair, threading his fingers through it until his hand lay against her neck. She quivered, melting, soft inside, and looked at him, her eyes wide and vulnerable.

'Can't we try again?' he murmured as with a groan of anguish he pulled her into his arms. 'Come back with me, Anna. You belong to me...I need you.'

She closed her eyes, longing to believe him and lose herself and the pain in the magic he offered. How easy it would be to do as he asked and go back.

But to what? Their life as it had been before? The loneliness, the waiting for him to come home, the company, and false friendships, and, of course, Sarah always there in the background like an intrusive shadow.

She pulled away and put the length of the room between them, unable to think rationally when he was so close, knowing that right now she must use her head and not her heart.

'Why, Matt?' she asked. 'You don't really need me. You are the most self-sufficient man I know.' She shook her head as he opened his mouth to speak. 'No, let me finish. I know you hate failure more than anything, and my leaving you has hurt your pride. Is this why you want me to come back? So we can present a picture of married bliss before your family and friends?' She shook her head. 'Don't forget I saw you with Sarah. You should have married her, Matt. She's so obviously right for you that it makes *me* feel like an intruder when we're together.'

'That's crazy.'

'No, it's not, it's how I feel. I know she wants you. I also know that while she's around there isn't any hope for our marriage.'

His hands clenched into fists and he turned on her, his face a dark mask of anger. He gripped her arms, careless of his fingers bruising her soft flesh as he dragged her against him. She gasped, shocked by the savagery in his eyes.

He ground his mouth down on hers and she struggled to free herself. But he was too strong, her struggles were futile and only aroused his desire for her. She felt the thrusting power of his hips and thighs and went limp in his arms.

It was too late. He laughed triumphantly and she shuddered, feeling the strong heat of her own blood pounding, the fire in her body taking over, drowning resistance...

'Please,' she gasped. 'Please don't... It's too late... It's over.'

He smiled wolfishly and moved his hips against her, keeping her body prisoner within his arms, pressed close, his thigh moving between hers.

He kissed her mouth with passion, his tongue tasting her, igniting her desire until she writhed helplessly against him, her fingers weaving themselves through his hair.

His hand slipped beneath her shirt and found her breast, hard fingers teased the taut nipple, and she whimpered impatiently, wanting, needing to feel him against her.

'You really believe it's over?' he asked hoarsely. 'Do you, when I can make you want me like this?' His hand cupped her cheek and he outlined her mouth with his thumb, gently probing her lips. She tasted salt on his skin and inhaled the musky, masculine scent of him, and her body throbbed with longing.

'Do you?' he repeated.

She opened her eyes and saw herself reflected in the dark intensity of his pupils, and knew it would be so easy to lose herself in him. He slid his hands to her hips, holding her close, moving on her, and she felt his need. 'Oh, Matt...' she murmured, weak and pliant in his arms.

Then they heard the stairs creak and Kate's voice calling from the kitchen.

'Hell!' Matt muttered eloquently and, releasing Anna, moved hastily through the french window and out of sight. Anna straightened her shirt and rubbed a hand across her mouth, a smile already on her lips as her gran came into the room.

'Oh, there you are,' she said. 'Where's Matt? Have you both had breakfast?'

'Matt's gone out for a walk, and yes, we've had breakfast,' Anna said breathlessly, half of her feeling bitterly disappointed by the interruption, the other half realising she'd had a lucky escape. She smiled. 'Come on, I'll get yours for you. What would you like?'

'Just toast and coffee, love, thank you. You two must have woken early this morning.'

'Yes, we did,' Anna agreed lightly. 'Matt's always up at the crack of dawn. It's a habit he got into while working in the field for the company.'

'A good habit too,' Kate remarked. 'I can't be doing with folk who lie in bed half the day... Well, would you believe it? Just look at that.'

She pointed to the back door, where the tabby cat was sitting as though he owned the place. He stretched and, walking boldly into the kitchen, sat down by the sink, staring expectantly at them through pale amber eyes while Webster growled indignantly from his safe perch on top of the fridge.

Anna laughed. 'Good morning, puss. Are you hungry?' She put milk down in a saucer, watching as he lapped delicately. Dry, he was no less scruffy than when she had pulled him out of the river. He was thin and scraggy, with matted fur and bald patches on his ears and tail. 'You are a sorry sight, aren't you?'

'It's probably covered in fleas. If it's staying, it'll have to have some of that spray I got from the vet. I can't have fleas in the house,' Kate said firmly.

'We'll call him Moses,' said Anna.

'Very original,' came Matt's voice from the doorway. 'Good lord, Kate, you're not letting her keep that mange-ridden animal in the house, are you?'

Anna glanced up, hating herself for the swift rush of pleasure she felt at the sight of him. He was laughing at her, his dark eyes sending secret, sensual messages across the kitchen.

She frowned. 'What would you suggest we do, throw him back in the river?'

He didn't reply but walked across to stroke Webster. 'Not good enough, is it, fella? You ought to stand up for your rights.'

'Oh, come on,' Anna laughed.

'I've a soft spot for old Webster, he did me a favour once and you don't forget your friends in their hour of need.' He took a fresh bottle of milk and poured the cream into Webster's bowl. 'There you are, pal, tuck in.'

'What are you two going to do today?' Kate asked brightly, thus effectively, Anna realised, bracketing them together as a couple again.

'It might be nice if we spent some time together,' said Matt.

Anna looked at his bland, smiling face and wished she could think of something suitably crushing to say. Whose fault was it they'd hardly been together in the first place?

'How about a picnic on the moors?' she suggested sweetly, knowing he hated eating outdoors.

'That's a great idea. How about you, Kate?' he asked.

She laughed. 'Count me out. I'm having tea with Ellen Whitacker this afternoon.'

'Then it'll be just the two of us.'

Anna sighed, realising she had been neatly out-manoeuvred. 'I'll look forward to it.'

Matt packed the picnic basket after lunch, though he refused to tell Anna what was in it. 'It's a surprise,' he said mysteriously.

As it happened, the sky clouded over and they only went as far as the stone bridge. Anna wondered if he chose this place deliberately, to evoke old memories. There were so many memories, stretching like bright threads between them, binding her to him.

They left the basket beneath the arch of the bridge to keep cool, and climbed a little way up Crossthwaite Moor. The path was a narrow sheep trail, steep and rocky in places, and Matt gave her his hand.

It felt good to cling to him, to feel him close. Right now, at this moment, she knew she was happy just to be with him.

They reached a rocky outcrop and stopped to rest, looking back across the moor. The breeze blew warm and peaty against their hot faces and somewhere near by they could hear the trickle of a spring.

Matt sat on a flat rock and pulled Anna down beside him, putting his arm around her, holding her close against his side.

'This is good,' he said softly. 'Away from pressures and people.' He glanced at her. 'That's the problem, isn't it, Anna?'

'What do you mean?'

'There are too many people around us. We spend our lives pretending, pleasing people, saying things they want to hear. How could we hope to get to know one another when we're too busy acting a part for the crowd?' He laughed. 'This morning you asked me if I'd noticed you don't eat breakfast. A simple thing, you might think, but it's an example of what our lives have become. We aren't real any more. We go through the motions of living, but none of it is real.' He waved his free arm wide to encompass the moor spread out before them. 'This is real.'

Anna couldn't think of anything to say, though she understood what he meant.

He smiled, hugging her against him. 'I reckon you and I lost touch with reality somewhere along the way. We lost sight of the things that matter. Maybe we should get back to basics, Anna, get back to the things that matter.'

'Do you think we can do that?' she asked softly. Far above them a hawk hung against the sky, swooped then hovered again, its wings beating the wind as it scanned the moor for prey, wild and free.

Matt watched the hawk too, his face inscrutable. 'I don't know. It depends on what we want out of life, doesn't it?'

'What do you want?' She held her breath, knowing his answer was of vital importance to her.

'I think you know the answer to that,' he said. 'I want you to come back to me, it's as simple as that.' He looked into her eyes. 'I want you back, Anna.' He rose quickly to his feet, dismissing the moment. 'Come on, race you to the bridge.'

Anna followed him, wishing her emotions would allow her to be objective, but it was impossible of course. She loved him and she wanted nothing more than to be with him, but it wasn't as simple as that. She knew she couldn't live with him on his terms, which was all he had to offer. He wanted her sexually, but it wasn't enough—they'd proved that already.

He unpacked the picnic basket on to a plaid rug beneath the willows beside the river. Cold chicken and salad, strawberries, and a bottle of champagne. Anna stared at the feast, memories slamming her like hammers.

Their honeymoon in the Greek Islands when they'd had strawberries and champagne on their wedding night, a picnic almost like this in their hotel bedroom...

'Where did you get these things at such short notice?' she demanded, feeling again that he had outmanoeuvred her.

'Out of the boot of the car,' he said innocently. 'Isn't that where everybody keeps their champagne?' He removed the cork and poured the bubbling liquid into glasses.

She accepted a glass with a sigh of resignation. 'You try hard, I'll give you that much.'

He laughed softly. 'You can't blame me for that, surely?'

Shrugging, she relaxed and helped herself to a piece of chicken. 'No, I don't blame you. I've been with you long enough to know that when you want something you tend to be single-minded about going after it.'

'It's the only way to be.' He raised his glass in a toast. 'What shall we drink to? The future, new beginnings?'

Anna shook her head. 'How about better understanding?'

'Sounds fine to me.'

She glanced away from him. 'Matt, don't expect too much of me too soon, please. Let's stand back from this a while, give ourselves some breathing-space.'

'OK,' he agreed. 'On your terms, Anna. Whatever you want. Strawberries?'

He handed her a glass dish filled with the shiny red fruit. They were sweet and luscious and he watched her bite into one, his eyes on her mouth making her feel self-conscious.

A drop of juice ran down her chin. He reached out and caught it, then licked his finger, still without taking his eyes from her face. She shivered and looked away, but he still watched her as the small space between them grew fraught with tension.

'Please, don't do that,' she muttered finally. 'Stop looking at me like that.'

'Why? I like looking at you,' he replied softly, smiling.

He picked a strawberry from her bowl, dipped it into his champagne glass, then fed it to her. Then leaned across and touched his mouth to hers, lightly, erotically tracing the shape of her lips with the tip of his tongue.

She closed her eyes, feeling the warmth of his champagne-scented breath mingling with hers as his mouth continued to caress and explore, feeling herself joined to him completely, irrevocably through this small, yet utterly sensitive contact even though he didn't touch her in any other way.

Finally he drew away, leaving her devastated, trembling, shattered, and began to gather the remains of their picnic together.

'It looks like rain,' he said conversationally. 'We'd better be getting back to the mill.'

Anna glanced up at the lowering sky with surprise. She hadn't noticed the gathering clouds. They ran back to the mill, but were still drenched by the downpour which started as they left their picnic spot. Matt covered them both with the rug and it flapped out behind them as they ran awkwardly together, splashing through puddles, ducking beneath low-hanging willows.

Lightning flashed and she clung to him with a small scream and then they were inside the mill kitchen, breathless, laughing. Then not laughing as they faced one another across the table, the memory of that kiss still between them.

Anna was the first to turn away. 'We'd better put the rug to dry before it shrinks——'

'To hell with the rug!' Matt muttered. In two steps he was across the kitchen and she was in his arms. And they both heard the front door open and Kate's footsteps in the hall.

Matt threw up his hands in despair. 'Dear lord, I can't stand much more of this!' he said in a tense whisper. 'I love Kate very much, but you have to admit her timing's lousy.'

'That depends on your point of view,' Anna replied.

'Right now, there is only one point of view, and you know it!'

Kate came into the kitchen carrying her outdoor shoes. 'It's throwing it down out there. I got soaked just coming from the car.' She looked at them standing in embarrassed silence on the far side of the table. 'Did you manage to have your picnic?'

Anna reached for the kettle and put it on to boil. 'Yes, we got back a few minutes ago.'

'We were just about to go up and get out of these wet things,' Matt added.

Anna dared not look at him. 'You go first,' she said hastily. 'I'll make some tea.'

'Good grief. . . tea!' he muttered, and slammed out of the kitchen.

Kate glanced after him. 'Have you upset him again?'

'Of course not, and why do you always assume *I* upset *him* when it's usually the other way round?'

'He looks a bit fraught, that's all. You have to understand, Anna, men are funny creatures.'

'Now she tells me,' Anna laughed. 'How is Mrs Whitacker?'

'Ah, that's what I wanted to speak to you about,' said Kate. 'Ellen's asked me to go to Benidorm with her, for a month.'

'What?' Somehow, Anna couldn't imagine her gran in the Spanish holiday resort.

'She was going with her sister, you know, the one who lives in York, but apparently she's gone down with shingles, poor thing. Ellen doesn't want to go to Spain on her own, so she asked me if I'd be interested. What do you think?'

'Do you want to go?'

'I think so. I could do with a holiday, but I can't quite make up my mind. Spain is very hot, isn't it? I'm not sure if I'll be able to stand the heat.'

'Of course you will,' Anna said briskly. 'We can go shopping tomorrow for some suitable clothes. I can look after things here, so you go off and have a great time with Mrs Whitacker.'

It wasn't until later that Anna realised her gran's departure would mean she'd be alone at the mill with Matt, but that was something she'd have to play by ear, always supposing he gave her time to draw breath, which wasn't likely in his present mood. And, despite her reservations, she felt a thrill of excitement at the prospect.

As for Matt, after the afternoon of the picnic he withdrew behind his own lines and left her severely alone, though on odd occasions she would find him looking at her, a strange expression in his dark grey eyes. Anna didn't trust him and wondered just what was going on in his mind.

Somehow, they managed to get Kate packed and ready to leave with Mrs Whitacker on the appointed day. Doug drove them to the airport and, when he called at the mill to collect Kate, he and Matt greeted one another with polite indifference.

When they'd gone, Matt said, 'I don't like your friend, what's-his-name.'

'His name is Doug, and you don't have to like him, do you?' Anna replied with a shrug.

'Maybe not, but I'm not too sure I like the way he looks at you. I think the guy fancies his chances.'

'For heaven's sake, Matt, he's a friend, nothing more—not that it's any of your business...'

His eyes glittering dangerously, Matt smiled. 'Ah, my love, but it is my business—for now, at any rate.'

'I've told you, Doug and I have been friends for years. You're just jealous,' she said lightly, suddenly very much aware that they had the house to themselves.

'So I'm jealous, I admit it, but I still don't like your friend Doug.' Then, as if reading her thoughts, he laughed and reached out his hand to her. 'Come and sit with me. Just think, we're alone at last.'

She sat beside him on the sofa. 'Just because we're alone it doesn't mean you can take liberties.'

He kissed the soft skin below her ear. 'What a deliciously old-fashioned remark. Besides, who said anything about taking? I think you're going to be giving, quite freely, my love.'

She drew away from him. 'Am I your love, Matt?'

'What do you think?'

'I know what I want to think, but that's not always the same thing, is it?'

'Will it make you feel better if I say, I love you?'

'Only if it's true.'

'Ah, there you have it, that one great big "if".' He settled her comfortably beside him, his arms around her. 'The difference between what I say, and what you believe. You don't trust me.'

It was a statement, not a question. 'No, I don't trust you,' she said frankly. 'How can I?'

His face was expressionless as he said, 'What will it take to make you trust me again, I wonder?'

She shook her head. 'I don't know, Matt. Time perhaps.'

They sat in silence for a while, then he said, 'Do you remember the first time I took you to Ashley Park?'

She smiled. 'How could I forget? There I was expecting to see a gracious old house in rolling parkland...'

'And you were faced with horror-movie Gothic, a monument to all the worst excesses of Victorian architecture.'

'But nice in its own way, once one gets used to it,' she added. 'And you have to admit it's in keeping. All that red plush and mahogany, and the flock wallpaper, and those dreadfully morbid paintings of dead animals.'

Matt chuckled. 'Somebody once described Ashley as a cross between a chapel of rest and a public library. Mother was not amused.'

Anna could imagine. Before meeting Estelle for the first time, Matt had said, 'Be yourself, darling, they'll love you.' Which hadn't helped at all.

Perhaps he'd known how his mother would react to her; the shocked surprise when he'd said they were to be married, quickly masked by a smile and one of those courtesy kisses that had pecked the air around Anna's right ear. Then the inquisition about her family background and the strained expression on learning that she was part-owner of a gift shop and made embroideries for a living.

To give her her due, Estelle had recovered her composure instantly, and had murmured, 'How fascinating,' before ringing for tea in the best English tradition.

She had soon discovered that Matt's two elder sisters were very much like their mother: aloof, snobbish and incredibly narrow-minded. Of the three only Matt had succeeded in following his own inclinations.

He worked for his uncle, it was true, but as Anna had got to know him better she'd realised that his position as the company's chief geologist had been achieved by his own efforts; his pride wouldn't let him presume upon his relationship with James Barratt.

Matt wasn't particularly ambitious, unless one counted his determination to succeed at whatever he tried to do, not in competition with anyone else, but against himself and his own limitations.

She had seen this side of his nature one weekend at Ashley not long after they were married, with the horse.

'Do you remember the first time you rode that half-broken horse of your mother's?' she said now.

'You mean Khan?'

Anna nodded. 'You were determined to ride him. I'd never seen such a crazy-looking animal and I was scared stiff you'd be killed. And angry that you could put yourself in such danger.'

'It wasn't that bad, Anna,' he protested.

'It was from where I was standing. I still feel sick when I think about it.'

She supposed it had taken courage to ride the horse, but she had tasted bitter fear as she watched him canter away down the drive. Her love had been so new and vulnerable, and, while Matt had looked romantic in his skin-tight jodhpurs, his dark hair ruffled by the wind, this new facet of his personality had filled her with insecurity.

On later visits, Anna had ridden one of the gentler mounts from Estelle's stables, not because she particularly enjoyed riding, but because she didn't want to be left behind when Matt took Khan out. And, also, because very often Sarah had been there, almost as daredevil as Matt, and with a recklessness she knew he admired.

But it hadn't made any difference. Sarah was always there, and Anna had been left behind in the end.

She felt a sudden chill and shivered.

Matt's arms tightened round her. 'Are you cold? Shall I fetch your sweater?'

She shook her head. 'No, I'm OK, thanks.' But the thoughts of Sarah had destroyed the moment of closeness. 'I'm tired—I think I'll go up to bed.'

She rose to her feet without meeting his eyes, but he clung to her hand. 'Is it any use my asking if I can come too?'

'No... not tonight, Matt.' She looked at him, hoping for understanding, but his face wore a closed look.

He shrugged. 'OK.'

She left him sitting there, feeling tears sting her eyes.

* * *

Matt watched her go, wondering what had caused her to suddenly withdraw into herself. Surely not the memory of himself riding that damned horse?

He shook his head, feeling helpless, not knowing where all this would end. He knew what he wanted, but right now his own needs didn't seem all that important.

He sighed wearily and, after allowing Anna time to get to her room, followed her up the stairs to spend yet another night in Kate Marshall's spare bed.

CHAPTER SIX

A WEEK passed. Seven days during which Anna and Matt seemed to be walking a tightrope, a careful balancing act, with no looking forward or back. It was enough to get through now, today, without any violent emotional demands one way or the other. And, though this bland state of affairs was at least comfortable, Anna had the sense to know it was merely a postponement and solved nothing.

Matt remained a friendly, caring companion—funny, witty, interesting himself in everything Anna wanted to do. They talked a lot, but within clearly defined limits, and all the time she felt the weight of the unsaid words creating its own barrier between them.

They drove to the coast on the Sunday, and as they mingled with tourists, exploring narrow streets and antique shops, Anna felt closer to Matt than she had for a long time.

They laughed together, ate ice-cream cones on the beach, joined in a game of football with a group of small boys, and walked barefoot along the edge of the water. Matt held her close to his side and she clung to him, her arm around his waist, feeling his strength, breathing in his warm masculine scent.

Anna felt relaxed and happy as they drove home. At that moment the barrier between them seemed almost transparent, as though all she had to do was reach out and it would disappear.

She looked at Matt and he smiled, and, tentatively, she touched his hand where it rested on the gear-lever, and he curled his fingers round hers and gently drew her hand to his lips without taking his eyes from the road.

'What are you thinking?' he asked.

She leaned back in her seat with a contented sigh. 'I was thinking about how much I enjoyed today and what a pity it has to end.'

He turned the car into a lay-by and stopped. Dusk had fallen and the air drifting in through the open windows was warm and scented with hay and melting tarmac, smells familiar to Anna from countless trips to the sea with Kate when she was a small child.

Matt twisted in his seat until he faced her, his features blurred by the gathering darkness. She felt his hand touch her cheek and pressed against it, loving the contact of his smooth hard skin against hers.

'It doesn't have to end,' he said softly.

She smiled her understanding and shook her head. 'It's been a lovely day, Matt, like a dream. Only dreams don't last, do they?'

His fingers moved to cup the back of her head. 'You, Anna, my girl, are a pessimist. You need a lesson in positive thinking.'

'I'm not a pessimist!' she cried. 'I'm just cautious. You know the old saying, once burned . . .?'

'There's another old saying, he or she who hesitates is lost, and I think maybe you and I have done enough hesitating just lately.'

Gentle pressure brought her nearer; she felt his warm breath on her cheek and, with a feeling of inevitability, she closed her eyes as his mouth brushed lightly across hers.

'You ought to know by now that I'm not a patient man. You've kept me at arm's length for a week, but you realise we can't go on like this, don't you?' He moved away from her again and she was aware of sharp disappointment.

And, as if sensing it, he laughed. 'I think you do realise it, my sweet Anna. And, though you'd rather die than admit it, I also think that you're finding our present state of polite celibacy just as much of a strain as I am.'

Anna was glad of the darkness as her face burned hotly. Was she so transparent, or was it that he knew her so well? Neither option was particularly comforting at that moment, when she was forced to acknowledge the fact that Matt was right.

'It's not that simple,' she said.

'Things are as simple or complicated as we make them,' he replied frankly. 'This past week we've talked up and down and around the one subject we needed to talk about, namely, our relationship and its future.' He took a deep breath. 'We have two choices, my love. We either cut and run, or we stay together and make it work.'

'This is a marriage we're talking about, not a company merger,' Anna protested, hating his coolly impersonal tone.

'I know that, dammit, but it won't help us if we get all uptight and emotional about things at this stage. We have to be objective.'

'Oh, my goodness,' Anna muttered under her breath. 'All right, be objective. Talk, convince me you're right and I'm wrong.'

'Well, the way I see it we have to evaluate what we have as opposed to what we'd like to have, and come to some kind of compromise. That's always supposing we stay together.'

'Oh, yes, I agree,' Anna said drily. 'Compromise is always the best solution. It usually means I fall in with what you want and you continue to do as you like, doesn't it?'

He sighed. 'We're not going to get anywhere if you take that attitude.'

'Oh, sorry. I didn't realise we were being serious about this.'

'Of course we're being bloody serious. Now, where was I?'

'Compromise,' she reminded him sweetly.

'Ah, yes. Well, in the plus column, we like one another's company, don't we? You don't find me boring?'

'No, you're definitely not boring,' she agreed. 'Quite the opposite, in fact.'

'And I am reliable. You have to admit that much.'

'In what way?'

'I'm in regular employment, you've never starved. I've never kept you short of money.'

'That doesn't count. I never starved before I married you, either.'

'I always turn up on time.'

'To my knowledge you have at least half a dozen watches.' Anna sighed. 'Look, this is all irrelevant as far as I'm concerned. I didn't marry you because you were punctual, or had a good job. I married you because I loved you.'

'Loved, past tense?' he asked lightly.

'As I said before, things aren't that simple any more.'

'Agreed, but nothing worth fighting for is simple. So, you take the bottom line and build on that.'

'What is the bottom line?' she asked quietly.

'You, me, the fact that I'm almost a hundred per cent certain you don't really want our marriage to end, and I'm damned sure I don't. That's enough to work on, isn't it, Anna?'

His voice was soft, persuasive. He took her hand and kissed the palm, and closed her fingers over the kiss.

Then he leaned across the small space between them and found her mouth unerringly in the darkness. 'We have too much to let go, my love,' he murmured against her lips. 'Say yes.'

She sighed and allowed herself to relax against him, giving in to the drugging pressure of his mouth, of his hands on her body. This was it, wasn't it, the bottom line? Compromise with him was preferable to a long, lonely life without him.

Somewhere inside herself a tiny voice protested her weakness, but she silenced it ruthlessly.

Although she didn't speak, Matt sensed that she had made her decision and smiled. He relaxed a little, though not too much. They weren't out of the wood yet, not by a long way. This new, tentative agreement between them could still tear itself apart if he didn't go carefully. But they had made a start. After all, he reasoned, every journey begins with the first step...

'Shall we go home?' he said. He could feel her, soft and pliant in his arms, feel his own desire for her growing more urgent. She pushed her hands inside his shirt, and as her fingers touched and explored his flesh quivered, wanting more, wanting her.

He shifted impatiently. The front seat of a car was way down on his list of the best places in which to make love.

He withdrew from her, reluctantly. 'Let's go home to bed.'

'Yes,' she replied, her voice as soft as a sigh in the darkness.

The phone was ringing when they reached the mill. Anna ran to lift the receiver, thinking it might be her gran calling from Spain.

Instead, a female voice said, 'Is that you, Mrs Tennant? This is Wendy Hope, Matt's secretary. Sorry to bother you so late, but would it be possible to speak to Matt?'

For a moment Anna was tempted to deny all knowledge of Matt's whereabouts, then thought better of it. There was a worried tone to Wendy's voice which meant something must be wrong.

Matt came into the room and she looked at him, feeling as though something precious was slipping away as she handed him the receiver.

'It's for you,' she said. 'Your secretary.'

'Hell! What does she want? It's Sunday, for heaven's sake.'

Anna shrugged. 'You'd better ask her.'

'Hello, Wendy—this had better be a matter of life and death,' he said tersely. 'I'm on holiday, remember.'

He listened intently, then, as though he had forgotten Anna was there in the room with him, he turned his back on her as he said, 'Any casualties?' Another pause and he added, 'Right, it'll take me about an hour to get to the airfield, if I push it.' He glanced at his watch. 'Tell them to expect me at around eleven o'clock, OK?'

He replaced the receiver and pushed his fingers through his hair distractedly. Then he looked up and saw Anna.

'There's been an explosion at one of the drilling sites I helped set up in Kuwait. People have been injured.' He gripped her arms tightly and bent to kiss her mouth. 'I'm sorry, Anna, but I have to go. There's no one else available who knows enough about it, you see. They're sending a company jet to pick me up from East Midlands Airport.'

She smiled. 'That's all right, I understand.' Inside she was protesting, surely in a company the size of Barratt

Oil there had to be someone else to take responsibility. But Matt was chief geologist, the Kuwait sites were his responsibility. 'How long do you think you'll be away?'

He shrugged. 'There's no way of knowing till I get there and assess the damage. But I'll be back as soon as I can, you can depend on that much. You and I have a little unfinished business and I'm not about to let you forget it.' He kissed her again and she clung to him, wishing he didn't have to go tonight.

'I hate leaving you here alone,' he said.

'I've been alone before. Besides I'll have Webster and Moses for company.'

'Will you be here when I get back?'

Anna nodded. 'I'll be here. I haven't anywhere else to go.'

Swallowing the knot of misery in her throat, she made coffee while he packed. Matt was used to travelling at a moment's notice and was ready to leave within fifteen minutes. She could tell he was impatient to be on his way, and was brisk and cool as they said goodbye. Until the last moment, when she clung to him and he held her tightly, his face buried in her hair.

Then he gently put her from him and, reaching into his pocket, produced a key on a little jewelled key-ring. 'This is yours,' he said, 'if you want to use it.'

It was her own key to the cottage, which she'd left behind. She held it close in her hand and smiled tremulously. 'Thank you.'

He touched her cheek, smiling. 'Mind you don't lose it again, OK?' With that, he turned abruptly and hurried out to his car, and it wasn't until she had watched the Jaguar's red tail-lights disappear along the lane that her tears broke through the tight shell of self-control.

* * *

Somehow Anna filled the hours. She cleaned the house from top to bottom, she spent each morning with Lucy at the shop, and she started on a new design for a tapestry picture commissioned by a previously satisfied customer. Three weeks, and by the Friday before Kate's return she had almost managed to convince herself she wasn't missing Matt.

Almost, but not quite. She still ran to pick up the phone whenever it rang, and would find herself watching avidly for the postman's van in the lane. Not that she expected Matt would have time to write to her, but...

She felt fidgety, unsure of herself. She had come back to Crossthwaite convinced that Matt didn't love her and that her marriage was finished for good. She went over their week together in her mind, reliving conversations, remembering the things he had said, and now she didn't know any more.

Inside herself hope had taken root and was growing stronger as the days passed. She looked at his picture on her dressing-table and felt a surge of joy which refused to be crushed by any pessimistic thoughts.

She had her key to their little house in London, and, though she knew she couldn't leave the mill until her gran returned from Spain, by Friday morning she was almost certain in her mind that she would go back and give her marriage another chance.

Sarah Barratt called to see her on Friday afternoon.

Anna answered the door to her ring and shock left her speechless for whole seconds.

Sarah smiled. 'Hello, Anna darling. Aren't you going to ask me in?'

Anna resisted the urge to slam the door in the other woman's face, and stepped back to allow her into the house. 'What brings you here? I thought you were in

California,' she said, keeping her voice carefully indifferent.

Sarah shrugged her slender shoulders. 'You know how it is. Things get so boring after a while. The same old people and places...' She was wearing skin-tight designer jeans and a red silk shirt, with a great many gold bangles which jingled when she moved her arms. Her long hair was tied at the back with a ribbon to match her shirt.

The picture of casual elegance, Anna thought sourly, feeling a mess in her denims and T-shirt.

'I'm on my way to York,' Sarah continued. 'A girl I was at school with has invited me to a weekend house party. It'll probably be incredibly dull, but one has to relieve the monotony somehow.' She smiled slyly. 'So, as I was almost passing your door, I thought I'd stop for a little chat, seeing as Matt isn't here. Have you heard from him, by the way?'

The question was innocently put and Anna took it at face value. 'Not yet,' she said, 'but I expect he'll phone as soon as he has time.'

Sarah examined her flawless fingernails. 'I spoke to him on the phone this morning before I left London. You'll be glad to know he's all right.'

Anna felt a quick, sick jerk inside but kept her face expressionless. 'Did he say how long he'll be away?' she asked.

'No, but you know Matt, he hates being pinned down to a timetable.' Sarah glanced around the sitting-room. 'Have you two managed to patch things up yet?'

Anna stared at her, hating the knowing look in her cool grey eyes. 'What do you mean?'

'Well, you did walk out on him in New York, didn't you? He was so mad about that.' She laughed. 'Wounded male ego and so on. Everybody knew about it, you see, and Daddy didn't help matters when he interfered.'

'I don't understand—what does it have to do with your father?'

'Well, you know how obsessive he is about this wholesome family image thing he wants the company to project.' She lowered her voice confidentially. 'Between you and me, Daddy is rather a puritan at heart. He has this idea that all his executives should not only *be* happily married, but be seen to be so, if you understand what I mean. Divorce is definitely taboo as far as Barratts' is concerned, and Daddy told Matt that if he didn't sort out his marriage problems he'd be out of a job, and Estelle's allowance would be cut.'

'But that's impossible. He wouldn't do that to his own nephew.'

'You don't know darling Daddy. He'd do it to me if I didn't fall in line.'

Anna thought of James Barratt, and realised he was quite capable of such ruthlessness.

But if Sarah was speaking the truth...? She deliberately closed her mind to such a possibility. It couldn't be true... Could it?

Sarah laughed mirthlessly. 'You don't believe me, do you?'

Anna shook her head. 'I'm finding it very hard to swallow. Would you like some tea?'

'That would be lovely, thanks.'

Sarah followed her into the kitchen and watched as she made tea and took biscuits and cake from the larder. 'How very civilised we are,' she remarked. 'You don't like me very much, do you, but you still offer me tea and cake.'

'I was brought up to be polite,' Anna said lightly. 'Even to people I don't like.'

Sarah's smile was cat-like, secretive. 'You never understood how it was with Matt and me, did you?'

Anna handed her her tea. 'What is there to understand? He is my husband, not yours.'

'He should have married me,' Sarah said. 'It was what Daddy wanted from the beginning. I grew up believing that Matt and I would be together.' Her eyes widened innocently. 'You don't mind if I talk about it?'

Anna sighed. 'Of course I mind, but I can see you're dying to tell me anyway.'

'When we were kids, it seemed as if it was just Matt and me against the rest of the family. My father couldn't give a damn because I wasn't a boy and it was natural that Matt and I should team up. We were so alike, you see. I loved him so much...' She paused, touching her fingers to her lips.

'Drink your tea before it gets cold,' Anna said, knowing Sarah was saying things she didn't want to hear, but knowing also that there was nothing she could do but just sit there and listen.

'I spent most of my holidays at Ashley,' she continued. 'I lived for the holidays, and the times I could be with Matt.'

It sounded like an unhealthy obsession to Anna, but she didn't say anything. This had happened so long ago, after all.

'We needed one another,' said Sarah. 'I grew up needing Matt, and it seemed as natural as breathing the first time he kissed me properly. It was as if we'd both been waiting for that moment. Do you understand?'

Anna nodded, feeling cold inside. Sarah was describing a relationship in which there was no room for outsiders, for people like herself.

'We planned to get engaged,' Sarah continued, 'but I was invited to stay with some of Daddy's friends in

Tokyo and it was too good an opportunity to miss.' She shook her head. 'Looking back, I suppose I should have refused the invitation. Matt didn't want me to go. Still, I had a great time with the Charlesworths in Tokyo and, when Daddy decided to expand into Japan, it was only natural that I should stay on and be part of the operation. I didn't see Matt for almost two years, though we wrote to one another every week. He writes such romantic letters,' she added dreamily, 'I was sure he would wait for me.' She shrugged and her eyes filled with tears. 'But he didn't, he married you instead, and when I came home I found you were expecting his baby. I saw him ... we talked. He said he still loved me and that he knew he'd made a mistake by marrying you. He promised that after the baby was born he'd ask you to set him free. But then the baby died...I knew he wouldn't leave you, not then.'

The silence after she'd finished talking seemed deafening to Anna. She rose to her feet and went to look through the window, and was surprised to see it had started to rain.

She closed her eyes. It had rained on her wedding-day—a freezing December downpour that had drenched the pink flowers on Matt's mother's hat, and made photographs outside the church an impossibility.

But Anna had been so radiantly happy that even the rain hadn't been able to spoil her day, as, with Matt's hand holding hers, she had been introduced to the hordes of Tennant and Barratt relations who had thronged to Crossthwaite parish church to look at the little nobody Matthew had chosen to marry. Had they all known about his relationship with Sarah?

Anna gripped her hands tightly together, aware of nothing but the pain inside her, a real physical anguish that left her paralysed, helpless. She looked at Sarah weeping quietly over her cup of cold tea and knew with certainty that what she had told her was the truth. No one could be that good an actress.

She made herself go back to the table. 'So, what are we to do?'

Sarah raised drowned eyes. 'I love him.'

'I love him too, but he's a person, not a toy to be argued over,' Anna said with a briskness she was far from feeling. 'And I think we'd better postpone any more talk until Matt comes back from Kuwait. All right?'

Sarah nodded, wiping her eyes. 'I feel better now we've talked. I wanted to hate you, I should hate you, but I don't. Is that strange?'

'No, it isn't. After all, we can't help any of this, can we? It's just another version of the wretched eternal triangle.'

Anna looked at the girl and felt pity for her, imagining how it must feel when the man you loved married someone else. She also felt pity for herself, knowing that, to Matt, she was second best, the intruder, the woman he must stay married to or lose his job. What a mess it all was.

Then Sarah began to sneeze violently. Anna offered a glass of water, and stood there feeling inadequate as the sneezing bout continued.

With her handkerchief jammed over her face, Sarah began to look round the kitchen and finally spotted Moses lurking beneath a chair.

'A cat!' she shrieked. 'Oh, no, get it out of here! I'm allergic to cats!' She grabbed her bag and ran out of the room, still sneezing.

Anna stared after her, feeling sudden hysterical laughter bubbling inside. It wasn't in the least funny, not at all, but she couldn't help it.

She followed Sarah from the kitchen in time to see her disappear through the front door, still sneezing.

'I...I must go,' she gasped. 'Th...th...thanks for the tea. Goodbye.'

A last thunderous sneeze and she was gone. Anna sat down on the bottom of the stairs and felt the laughter drain away as abruptly as it had begun, and she wrapped her arms around her body, shivering, sick, dizzy with despair.

Kate returned from her Spanish holiday to find Anna huddled miserably in the sitting-room, still feeling sick and ill. Anna had never been so pleased to see anyone, and allowed herself to be fussed over and put to bed with a hot-water bottle, though in reality she felt too weak to put up much of a fight anyway.

'It must be something I ate,' she moaned, thinking death might be a suitable alternative to how she was feeling at that moment.

'You'll be all right tomorrow,' said Kate briskly. 'And, if you're not, you'll have to see the doctor.'

'No need for doctors.' Anna shook her head then wished she hadn't as the room whirled crazily. 'I forgot to ask, how was Spain?'

'Hot and crowded,' Kate replied. 'It was an experience, I'll say that much. If I ever go again, I think it'll have to be out of season. I brought you some castanets.'

'How nice,' Anna murmured weakly.

The sickness grew steadily worse over the next few days until Kate finally insisted upon telephoning the doctor's surgery for an appointment. Anna drove herself into town in her gran's little car. Kate did offer to go with her, but she refused. After all, she wasn't that feeble, even though her face was tinged a pale shade of green.

It was raining when she emerged from the surgery. She hurried to the car park, her hands stuffed deep into her jacket pockets, her shoulders hunched against the cold drizzle running down her neck.

She shivered, feeling sympathy for the pigeons huddled unhappily on ledges above the street, and for anyone else obliged to be out in such lousy weather. And for herself, though on the face of it the wet splashing up the legs of her tights was the least of her problems.

Imagine getting pregnant at a time like this. It was almost laughable; a perfect manifestation of Murphy's Law.

Her gran was working in the pottery when she got back to the mill. Anna watched for a moment as her hands formed a ball of clay on the wheel into a perfectly symmetrical bowl shape.

'Well, what did the doctor have to say?' she asked, carefully lifting the finished bowl and putting it with others ready for the first firing.

'I'm pregnant,' Anna said baldly. 'About six weeks.'

Kate smiled as she selected another ball of clay from the bin. 'I thought as much. How do you feel about it?'

'I'm scared,' Anna told her frankly.

'That's understandable,' Kate agreed. 'But they did tell you after Daniel died that there was no reason why it should happen with another baby.'

'I know, but I'm still scared. I don't think I could live through that again . . .' Anna laid her hands protectively over her stomach, feeling again the terrible wrenching loss of her first baby. How could she bear it if it happened again?

But then, she thought, it was much too late for that kind of speculation. The deed was done and she'd have to go through with it, risks and all.

Then realisation hit her like a blow to the head. She was going to have a baby! Matt's baby. Their baby. A tiny, frail human being which, when he found out, would bind Matt to her with bonds of steel.

'You'll be going home now.' It was a statement, not a question.

Anna looked at Kate. 'I don't know, Gran. This doesn't change anything really, it just adds another dimension to the problem.' And she went on to tell her about Sarah's visit the previous Friday.

'The trouble-making little madam! You didn't believe her?'

'I don't know what to believe. I thought she was telling the truth, but now I've had time to think I'm not so sure.' She sighed. 'I don't know what to do, Gran.'

'Listen to me—as soon as Matthew gets back from Kuwait, you tell him about the baby. That'll sort Miss Sarah Barratt out once and for all.'

'But I don't want him to feel he has to stay with me just because I'm pregnant. If he does love Sarah——'

Kate shook her head in exasperation. 'Matthew is a strong-minded man, Anna; if he was in love with Sarah, he would have married her and not you. Can you honestly see him backing down before threats from her father? He'd have told him where to put his job.'

'He couldn't do that. Apparently James Barratt threatened to cut Estelle's allowance too. Matthew's father didn't leave her much money and she relies on her brother's support to keep Ashley going.'

'So, he's got his mother hanging on to him like a ball and chain as well. He has my sympathy, poor lad.'

Anna smiled. Trust her gran to get things right back into perspective.

Inside the house the phone was ringing. Without thinking, she lifted the receiver, then felt her knees buckle when she recognised Matt's voice on the line.

'Hello, Anna, is that you?'

'Yes—hello, Matt,' she replied shakily. 'Where are you?'

'The office. I just have to finish my report and I'll be on my way. Expect me around five this afternoon, OK?'

'Yes...yes, that'll be lovely.' What a trite thing to say, she thought, fruitlessly searching her brain for something clever and witty to add.

'You might sound a little more enthusiastic... Did you miss me?'

She laughed breathlessly. 'Not particularly. Did you miss me?'

'I'll let you know when I get there,' he growled.

Anna's pulses jerked. 'I'll look forward to it.'

His reply was a lecherous chuckle as he broke the connection.

Dinner, she thought, searching through the contents of the fridge without finding a great deal to inspire her. Tonight called for something a little special, though Matt preferred plain food simply cooked. She decided on his favourite fillet steaks with a salad, with pâté to start, and raspberries and cream for pudding.

'Matt's coming back tonight,' she told Kate, unable to stop herself from smiling. 'I'm going shopping for our dinner.'

'Well, don't bother to include me in your calculations,' Kate replied. 'I'm out this evening.'

Anna stared at her. 'You never said.'

'Do I tell you everything?'

'No, but... Listen, you don't have to leave us alone, you know, Gran. This is your house.'

Kate laughed. 'I arranged this before I went to Spain. I just forgot to tell you, that's all.'

Anna agonised for an hour over what to wear. Her rebellious self made her pause, asking, what did clothes matter anyway? She wasn't out to impress him, was she?

Finally, she chose a plain blue cotton dress with a flatteringly gathered skirt. She always looked good in blue and it was her favourite colour. She wore pearl studs in her ears and brushed her hair until it shone with soft gold lights. Scent at her pulse-points and a little makeup, then she stepped back to look critically at the whole effect in her long mirror.

Not bad, she thought. At least she *looked* cool and self-possessed, even if her insides were churning with nervous anticipation.

She watched the hands on the clock creep round to five. The food was all prepared and a bottle of wine opened ready in the dining-room, where the table was set for two, with a centrepiece of roses from the garden in a crystal bowl.

Five o'clock, five-thirty. She went to and from the front window, watching for the black Jaguar coming along the lane. Six o'clock and she began to panic. Suppose he'd had an accident? He always drove that damned car as if he were at Brands Hatch...

Then it was there, drawing up outside, and from her vantage-point behind the curtains Anna watched as Matt climbed out, stretched and stood for a moment staring at the house. Her heart thumped crazily, her mouth was dry and she wished she could run and hide as he opened the gate and began to walk along the path.

How beautiful he is, she thought hungrily. The breeze ruffled his dark hair and he looked tanned and fit. He was wearing brown cord jeans, a sleeveless white T-shirt and carried his suede jacket slung over one shoulder.

He rang the doorbell and Anna forced herself not to rush to answer it. She put what she hoped was a bland, friendly expression on her face, took a deep breath and opened the door.

CHAPTER SEVEN

MATT smiled. Did he realise just how devastating his smile could be? Anna wondered. Now, the force of it made her skin tingle as he said,

'Hello, Anna.' She stood there, unable to move as he stepped inside, ducking his head as always to avoid the lintel, and reached for her.

'Come here, you,' he growled, hugging her close. 'Lord, I've missed you...' He kissed her mouth lingeringly then held her away from him. 'You've no idea how much I've been longing to do that.' His eyes moved over her. 'You smell wonderful...you look fantastic.'

Anna laughed softly, reminding herself that to a man who'd just spent a week in the desert any woman would seem wonderful. 'You don't look so bad yourself.' Though on closer inspection she saw the strain of exhaustion in his grey eyes. 'How did it go in Kuwait?' she asked, gently leading the way into the sitting-room.

'It was a mess. They'd had a pretty bad explosion. We're not too sure how it happened yet, though my money's on a bomb of some kind.' He sat down on the sofa, his shoulders slumped. 'Some of the men were badly burned. A guy who was at university with me died...'

'Oh, Matt, I am sorry.'

He managed a small smile. 'These things happen. It just hits closer to home when it's someone you know well.' Rubbing his forehead with his fingertips, he added, 'Tom—he's the one who died—was married, with two small kids.' He reached out a hand to her. 'Come here and tell me what's been happening in the real world while I've been away. Hell, was it only a few weeks? Feels like a year.'

This was the moment to tell him about the baby, she realised afterwards as she sat beside him, feeling his arm tighten around her. Instead she said, 'Will you have to go back to Kuwait?'

'I'm afraid so, love. They're having an on-site inquiry starting in three days, and I have to be there.'

'Three days?' she echoed in dismay.

'I only came back to put in my preliminary report . . . and to visit my favourite woman.' He cupped her chin in his other hand and turned her to face him. 'Did you miss me?'

'You know I did,' she replied softly. She held him, pressing her face into his neck. 'Oh, Matt, I wish you didn't have to go away again.'

She heard him chuckle, 'That's an improvement anyway,' and raised her head to look into his eyes, feeling her love for him surge in her like a soft explosion.

'I mean it,' she said, knowing he'd never realise how much.

She could smell his distinctive musky scent: aftershave and something deeper, more exciting; and she could hardly tear her eyes away from his mouth, so well-shaped and sensuous, his teeth showing white and even when he smiled. His dark eyes were unfathomable, the lashes short and thick; his hair was attractively rumpled and she reached out to touch it, unable to stop herself.

'I think you do.' He kissed her mouth and she felt his tongue flicker against her lips, and with a small sigh she relaxed into him, revelling in the feel of him, of his hands holding her, touching her body.

Then he moved back a little. 'Just as a matter of interest, where is Kate?'

'She's out this evening and said not to wait up.'

Matt sighed with satisfaction. 'Don't worry, we won't.'

He lifted her to lie across him and her skirt slithered upward as his hand trailed along her thigh.

Anna giggled breathlessly. 'What about dinner? You have to eat first.'

'Do I?' His fingers continued their exploration and she gasped with pleasure. He knew her so well and each caress, each movement of his body on hers, added more flame to the fire burning inside her, until she quivered with need, lost, helpless, reaching up blindly to find his mouth.

'Please, Matt,' she murmured, feeling him move against her as his lips burned her throat.

'Please what? Tell me.' He kissed her hungrily. 'Tell me.'

'Please...I want you—now.'

He lifted her into his arms and she nestled against him, eyes closed, aware of nothing but her own mind-shattering need of him.

In her bedroom he undressed her gently, almost reverently, his hands and mouth bringing her almost unbearable pleasure as they began their journey of rediscovery over her body. And when he undressed and lay down beside her, she felt him tremble, felt the power of his need.

She looked into his eyes and saw uncertainty. Why was he hesitating? She touched his face with her fingertips, and he caught her hand and took it to his lips.

'Are you sure?'

'Yes, I'm sure.' She smiled, loving him, proud of the desire she saw in his dark eyes and felt in his body, which fitted so well with her own that they were like two halves of a whole, united, blended joyously by their love.

And then it was too late for regrets as with a soft sigh she felt the weight of him on her, and acknowledged the utter bliss of his loving, shared his triumph as they achieved perfection together, a total giving that shattered all barriers between them in an ecstasy of feeling.

Afterwards she lay quietly, her cheek resting against his damp skin, feeling the steady beat of his heart beneath her hand.

'That was beautiful,' he murmured. 'You are beautiful.' His arms tightened around her. 'We are good together, you and I.' He sighed, and moments later his even breathing told Anna he was asleep.

She propped herself up on one elbow and watched him as he slept, feasting her eyes, drinking in the sight of him in a way that was impossible when he was awake and aware.

Most of the time he was completely unselfconscious about his body, though there were occasions when he had seemed embarrassed to have her looking at him, almost as though he was unsure of himself in some way.

She had once told him he was beautiful, and he had laughed. 'Men are not beautiful,' he'd said.

'You *are* beautiful,' she whispered now, touching his chest lightly with her fingertips, encircling his flat male nipples and caressing down the line of dark hair to his belly.

She concentrated on the tactile pleasure of his flesh beneath her hands, keeping her thoughts firmly on here and now and deliberately ignoring the questions which nibbled at the edges of her mind.

His face was closed, vulnerable in sleep, and a tiny frown puckered between his brows. He sighed and nuzzled close into her breasts like a child seeking reassurance, and love and need surged in her.

If only it were that simple, she thought. If only her love were enough to smooth the way. He had wanted her, would want her again. As he said, they were good together sexually. But there was more to a marriage than sex, wasn't there? Things like trust and friendship and the need to be together mentally as well as physically.

Anna wanted all of Matt, but she had no way of knowing how much he was prepared to give, and half-measures were nowhere near enough.

She gently eased herself from the bed and stooped to cover him with the duvet, but he didn't wake and she realised he must have been exhausted.

In the bathroom she showered quickly and slipped into a loose blue silk caftan, then went downstairs to prepare dinner. Matt would be hungry when he woke, and Anna herself was feeling faint empty rumblings.

Pregnancy had an odd effect, she thought as she tossed the salad in a light dressing. She felt like death first thing in the morning but the rest of the time she was ravenous.

She frowned. Later, when they had eaten and Matt was properly relaxed, she would tell him about the baby, and she felt nervous at the prospect because his reaction would tell her once and for all how much truth there had been in Sarah's tearful revelations.

Matt appeared at the kitchen door just as she was putting the finishing touches to their meal. He had showered; his hair was rumpled and damp and he wore just a towel around his hips.

'I left my bag in the car,' he said, grinning.

She laughed. 'What a shame. Still, I heard that towels are just the thing for evening wear this year.'

He slid his arms around her and kissed her neck. 'Mmm, you smell delicious.'

'It's the steaks,' she replied flippantly. 'And stop that or you'll get no dinner.'

He chuckled wolfishly. 'Forget the dining-room. Let's eat upstairs.'

There was something wonderfully crazy about sitting cross-legged on her bed, washing the steak down with champagne. Matt ate hungrily, and they talked and laughed about nothing in particular, seemingly enclosed in a magic bubble of pleasure that had nothing at all to do with reality.

And, when they had finished, Matt shoved the tray of used dishes across the room with his foot, then lay down beside her, and kissed her mouth lingeringly.

He tasted of champagne and raspberries. His kiss was part of the magic, dreamlike, apart, and when he gently removed her caftan she put up no resistance and lay there, sighing with pleasure as he began to caress her body.

She closed her eyes, her hands exploring his smooth, warm skin. Then burying themselves in his hair as his lips found her breast and began to suck gently, his tongue rubbing teasingly across the sensitive peak. His hair brushed her skin, and she quivered as his mouth travelled further, downwards across her belly to the soft mound between her thighs.

Anna whimpered, writhing helplessly in the grip of a pleasure so intense she thought she might die of it.

Matt, sensing her reaction, smiled. 'You like...?' Her fingers dug into his flesh and he moved to kiss her breasts again, watching her face, playing her like a finely tuned instrument as he took his pleasure from hers and her touch on his body.

Then he could wait no longer. Mouths, tongues, bodies fused into one long, white-hot flare as he lifted her hips to meet him. Her softness enfolding him, her hands pressed hard against his skin, her head thrown back in an agony of ecstasy as they reached the summit together.

Then soft cries, pounding hearts, as the slowly receding tide of passion lapped against their helplessly entwined bodies.

He held her in his arms, pressed close into the curve of his body, and they both slept.

Anna woke slowly, her arm groping blindly across the empty pillow beside her own. She opened her eyes gingerly, then wished she hadn't as a grinding pain slammed through her temples.

Clutching her head in both hands, she crawled out of bed and just made it to the bathroom in time. Afterwards, she scrubbed her teeth and felt slightly better as she peered at herself in the mirror.

'Serves you right,' said her reflection smugly. 'All the books say that alcohol is bad for both you and the baby, so let this be a lesson!'

'Shut up,' she replied. 'All I had was one glass of champagne. That isn't enough to hurt anyone.'

'You know what they say about people who talk to themselves,' said Matt from the doorway.

Anna spun round guiltily. How much had he heard? Then she felt relief. He hadn't heard enough apparently, because he strolled over to her looking disgustingly healthy and wide awake, in blue denims and a sweatshirt with 'Malibu' across the front in bold black letters.

And, as she saw his eyes flick over her appreciatively, she realised she hadn't had time to grab her dressing-gown before her frantic dash to the bathroom. Still, it was too late now for modesty, she thought philosophically.

Matt touched her cheek gently. 'You look pale. Do you feel all right?'

'Yes, I'm fine,' she replied quickly, too quickly, though he didn't seem to notice as he slid his arms around her, resting his hands flat against her stomach.

'You've put some weight back on,' he murmured into her neck. 'I like that.' His hand caressed her hips and down the sides of her thighs. 'You have a gorgeous, sexy woman shape.'

She felt his hips pressing against her and turned in his arms. He kissed her mouth hungrily.

'Let's go back to bed.'

'No, we can't. What about Gran?' Anna whispered, laughing.

'Oh, for heaven's sake—I'm not asking you to have an illicit relationship. We are married.'

'I know, but . . . well, you know,' she said helplessly.

Matt sighed and let her go. 'Yes, I do know, and the sooner we get back home the better. I want to be able to make love to you when I want, not when some half-baked convention dictates.'

Anna bent to turn on the bath taps. It sounded as if he was taking it for granted they would go back home, together. She smiled softly. It was what she wanted, wasn't it?

Then she looked at Matt's sweatshirt, and knew it must have been a present from Sarah, perhaps after her most recent visit to the Malibu beach house, and she felt a cold shiver of foreboding touch her skin. Sarah had been in love with Matt for years. She wouldn't let him go that easily.

Kate was cooking breakfast when they went down-stairs. She greeted Matthew with enthusiasm and loaded bacon and scrambled eggs on to his plate.

Anna turned away from the nauseating spectacle and nibbled on a piece of dry toast. Kate caught her eye across the table, her brows raised in question as she mouthed, 'Did you tell him?' over Matt's head.

Anna shook her head slightly, frowning as she heard Kate's heavy sigh of exasperation.

She and Matt chatted over breakfast, though Anna was too busy holding on to her stomach to offer much by way of contribution to the conversation. Luckily, Matt was accustomed to the fact that she didn't eat in the mornings, so her lack of appetite didn't raise any comment.

'I'll see to the dishes,' she said when they'd finished.

'No, Matt only has today and tomorrow before he has to go back to Kuwait. You two go and have some time together. I'll see to what needs doing here,' said Kate firmly, with a further significant glance in Anna's direction. 'And if I'm not here when you get back don't worry. Ellen and I are going into town later and will probably make a day of it.'

'You heard the lady,' said Matt, taking Anna's hand and pulling her outside. 'Come on, you look as if you could do with some fresh air.'

Anna knew protests were useless with the pair of them against her, so with a little shrug of resignation she followed Matt down to the river.

The air was still and filled with freshness and birdsong. Matt began to skim stones across the smooth surface of the water, and for a few moments Anna allowed herself the pleasure of watching the play of his muscles as he stooped and threw. Then he turned and looked at her, but he didn't smile.

'It's decision-time, Anna,' he said. 'I want to know if you'll be home when I come back from Kuwait next time.'

She looked at him, unable to speak.

Matt shrugged. 'It's a reasonable question, don't you think?'

She turned away from his penetrating grey eyes. 'I...I don't know.'

'What do you mean, you don't know? After last night I shouldn't have thought there'd be any doubt.' He pushed his hand through his hair. 'Good lord, what do I have to do, get down on my hands and knees, grovel, tear out my soul and hand it to you on a plate?' He gripped her hands tightly. 'Anna, we made beautiful love last night. Didn't it mean anything to you?'

'Did it mean anything to you?' she countered, amazed she could sound so matter-of-fact when it felt as if she was clinging to a cliff by her fingertips, with a bottomless void below her feet.

'It proved we're still good together,' said Matt.

'In bed, yes, but there's more to life than sex.'

He laughed mirthlessly. 'Is there?'

She stared at him. 'You know there is.'

'I wonder, Anna, my love. We were together for a year and a half and we enjoyed one another for most of that time. We could go on enjoying. I'm not ready to give you up, and I don't think you really wanted to leave me. You just let stupid suspicions cloud your judgement.'

'Stupid suspicions?' she echoed hotly. 'It was more than that, and you know it!'

He shrugged. 'OK, I was stupid too. I should have seen the way things were heading and used a little tact and understanding, especially after the baby... But you know me, I'm not too good at the diplomacy bit. If I want to say or do a thing, I go ahead and damn the consequences. It's the way I am. I haven't the patience to go pussy-footing around saying one thing when I mean another. You married me as I am and I see no reason to pretend to be something different.'

'But we do change,' Anna protested. 'We can't help it. Time and circumstances make us into different people whether we like it or not.'

'Only if we let them,' he said quietly. 'If you hadn't had the baby I don't think anything would have changed for us.'

'I don't understand. We planned to have a family. We wanted the baby.'

'Correction. You wanted the baby.'

She stared at him. 'Don't give me that! You were as happy as I when I became pregnant so soon after we were married.'

He sighed. 'I was happy because you were. All I wanted was for you to be happy.' He held his arms wide. 'Didn't you know I'd have given you the moon if I could get it down from the sky? A baby was easy by comparison.'

Anna felt cold to the bone. 'You didn't want our baby?'

'At the beginning, no, I didn't. I had all I wanted in you.' He raised his brows. 'Am I selfish, or merely uncomfortably honest? I don't have any dynastic ambitions. I'm not so filled with arrogant conceit that I wish to see myself perpetuated in the faces of more sprigs on the Tennant family tree. I didn't yearn for fatherhood. I married you, Anna, because I loved you, because my life was empty when you were not there, because I thought we could make one another happy. I wanted you for my wife, my lover, my friend, companion, but not necessarily to be the mother of my children.'

He turned away to stare across the river to where a pair of swans swam protectively around a group of half-grown cygnets. 'Then, when you became pregnant I was scared, I didn't want anything to change for us, though I knew it must.' He smiled wryly. 'Maybe it took me that long to grow up. Each day I watched you become more beautiful and found myself looking at other people's children and I imagined us doing all the things they did, you know, the trips to the zoo and stuff like that...'

Anna's eyes stung with tears as he looked at her. 'I didn't know... You never said....'

'Oh, Anna, I mourned our child, I still do. Inside me there's an ache that won't go away, I feel anger and frustration because this terrible thing happened to us. I loved Daniel. He was part of us and he existed... If he had lived...' He shook his head. 'But he didn't live, and, in dying, it seemed he took everything we had.'

Anna was shocked to the core. She had never dreamed he felt this way. But then, she had never stopped to question his feelings on the matter, had she? She had taken them for granted, never realising all this was going on behind his smiling face.

And given his attitude, how terrible it must have been for him afterwards when, in her grief, she had withdrawn into herself and refused to allow him near her.

And how understandable that in his rejection he should turn to Sarah for comfort. She thought of the new baby growing inside her and knew that, with the sharp memory of so much sadness hanging between them, this wasn't the moment to tell him about it.

'I didn't know,' she said humbly. 'Why didn't you tell me?'

'Would you have listened?' he asked bitterly.

There didn't seem anything more they could say. Silently, each wrapped in thought, they turned and walked back to the house.

Kate's Mini was gone from the yard, but there was a small red hatchback parked in front of the house behind Matthew's Jaguar, and Anna's heart sank as she recognised the car Sarah had been driving the previous Friday.

As they approached, Sarah climbed out and waved to them, smiling.

Matt swore softly. 'What the hell is she doing here?'

'Hi, there you are,' Sarah called. Her voice was low and melodious and as she came nearer Anna saw she was beautifully dressed in a jade-green silk suit, and her long hair was taken into a smooth chignon that showed off the delicate bone-structure of her face to the best advantage. A definite contrast to how she had looked last time she had visited the mill.

'Matt, darling, I was hoping to catch you,' she cried, reaching up to kiss his cheek. She glanced at Anna. 'Hello, Anna, you're looking well.'

Anna felt dull and plain beside such perfection and hated herself for her own feelings of inadequacy. Her answering smile felt wooden as she said, 'Hello, Sarah, this is a surprise.'

'You remember I told you I was on my way to a weekend house party in York?' she said. 'Well, it was just as deadly dull as I anticipated.'

'What a shame,' Anna replied ironically. 'I do hope you recovered from your allergy reaction to the cats.'

'As soon as I got outside I was fine. It's too silly for words.' Sarah's laugh was high and brittle and Matthew looked from one to the other, without a clue as to what they were talking about.

'What do you want?' he demanded rudely.

'I knew you were here, darling, so I thought we could drive back to London together.'

He nodded towards the red car. 'And what do you propose to do with that thing—tow it behind?'

She laughed again. 'Of course not. It's rented and the hire company can collect it from here just as easily. You don't mind, do you, Anna?'

'Just hold your horses there, Sarah,' Matt said brusquely. 'It just so happens I'm not driving back until tomorrow. Where do you intend to spend the night?'

'Oh, but we have to be in London tonight. Didn't you know?'

He stared at her. 'You're joking. I only arrived home yesterday.'

Sarah shrugged. 'Daddy phoned me last night and I naturally assumed he'd been in touch with you too. Apparently, a couple of opposition MPs are flying out for a meeting with some high-ranking members of the Kuwait government and they plan to visit the oil field on a fact-finding mission, in view of the British casualties in the explosion. Daddy's furious, of course. He wants you back immediately to deal with the situation.'

She didn't sound over-bothered, Anna thought. She looked at Matt and saw his face was white and strained beneath the tan.

'Why the panic?'

'They think it was a terrorist bomb. A couple of explosives experts will be flying out with you. The jet is standing by for tonight.'

They had moved into the house as Sarah explained the situation to Matt. As though she had never seen it before she glanced around the sitting-room and smiled vaguely at Anna.

'Lovely room.'

'Thank you. Would you like some coffee?'

'I'd love some.' Sarah sat gracefully on the sofa. 'I'm shattered after that bloody house party.'

'Poor you,' Matt said sarcastically.

Anna left the room, unable to bear the sight of them together—Sarah, so elegant and lovely, Matt leaning over her and, in spite of his tone, gazing as if he couldn't take his eyes off her.

In the hall she paused, listening unashamedly at the door like someone probing an open wound.

'Your coming here was rather tactless, under the circumstances,' she heard Matt say.

'It seemed sensible for us to travel together, especially as Daddy told me I'll be flying out with you tonight.'

'You're what? Like hell you are! Has he finally lost his marbles? Hasn't anybody told him it's bloody dangerous out there?'

'Calm down, darling. I won't be in any danger. I shall be staying in Kuwait City to deal with the Press, that kind of thing.'

'I still think it's a daft idea.'

'I had no choice, Matt. You know what Daddy's like.'

'I'm up to here with bloody Daddy!' Matt said viciously. 'I'd like to tell him where to stuff his damned job, and the company!'

'But you won't do that, will you?' Sarah was positively purring.

'Only because I'm needed at the field. Afterwards, I'm not so sure.'

'We'll see. I think I can get you to change your mind.' There was a soft, seductive chuckle and Anna clenched her fists in jealous rage, longing to scream and swear and smash things.

'By the way,' Sarah continued, 'how are you and Anna getting along?'

'Fine, if it's any of your business!'

'Don't be snappy, darling. I'm interested, that's all.'

'I can't imagine why!'

'Can't you? Come on, Matt, use your famous intelligence. Anna's weak—you should never have married her in the first place. I'll never understand why you did, because anyone with half an eye can see you have nothing in common.'

'Sarah, drop it. Believe me, now is not the time for this discussion!'

'You should have married me, Matt,' Sarah persisted. 'I would have been a much better wife for you. It would have been the perfect arrangement. We understand one another, you and I, we're two of a kind.'

Unable to bear any more, Anna crept into the kitchen. She was shaking and gripped the edge of the table tightly, breathing deeply as she fought for control.

She was afraid of the rage which burned through her. She wanted to kill Sarah; she wanted to kill them both. She made coffee and pondered on the possibilities of rat poison and ground glass, but had neither to hand, which was just as well.

She felt hysterical laughter bubbling inside her. It served her right for listening at doors.

Yet Sarah's words had struck at Anna like sharp hammer blows, crushing the frail hopes she had begun to nurture in her heart. How could she compete with the other woman when there was so much between them she didn't share? Matt and Sarah would fly away together tonight and as always Anna would be left behind.

But at least she could say goodbye with dignity, she decided, and tipping biscuits on to a plate she carried the tray through to the sitting-room.

They were both standing by the window and Anna found herself staring at Sarah's perfect make-up for signs of smudged lipstick, but she couldn't be sure. Matt looked at her, his expression unreadable as she handed Sarah her cup.

'Ah, you are an angel,' she cooed gratefully. 'You've no idea what a horrendous drive I had to get here. Roadworks and traffic jams all the way from York, not to mention busloads of tourists. I could never understand why so many people come to Yorkshire. After all, there's nothing here, is there?'

Anna looked at her. Sarah appeared as if she'd just left a beauty shop, gift-wrapped for Matthew in the uncrumpled silk suit which had probably cost more than Anna could earn in a year.

'It depends what you're looking for,' she said. She offered Matt a cup of coffee and he glared at her.

'Coffee? You must be joking!' he snapped and, moving to the drinks tray, helped himself to a double Scotch.

'Careful,' Sarah warned. 'Don't forget you're driving.'

'So?' he enquired nastily. 'Are you suggesting I can't hold my drink?'

'Don't go all macho, darling. I'm not suggesting anything of the kind. It's just that you don't want to risk getting stopped by the police and breathalysed, do you?'

'When I want your advice, I'll ask for it!'

Sarah sighed. 'Oh, dear. How do you put up with his bad temper, Anna? I think we'd better change the subject, don't you?'

She laughed prettily and Anna felt embarrassed. Matt was being abominably rude and for some reason she felt responsible, which was crazy. Why should she worry about his lack of manners?

He came to stand beside her and put his arm around her shoulders. She could smell the whisky on his breath.

She could also smell Sarah's scent on his clothes and felt the coldness of despair churning in her stomach.

'By the way, darlings,' said Sarah, 'before I forget, you must be the first to congratulate me on my engagement.'

There was a brief, dense silence. Anna felt Matt's body become rigid and his arm dropped away from her. Sarah smiled at him, clearly well satisfied with the playing of her trump card.

'Engagement?' he echoed hoarsely.

'Mmm, I thought you'd be surprised; that's why I've decided to tell you now although it's still supposed to be a secret. I didn't want you to hear the news from anyone else but me.'

'Who?'

Anna watched them both, feeling like a spectator at a play. Neither seemed aware of her presence as their eyes locked across the room.

Sarah laughed, thoroughly enjoying herself. 'I think you've met him, Matt. It's a friend of my father's— Andrew Klein.'

'Good grief, not the baked-bean king? He's had four wives already. You can't marry that lecherous old man!'

'Oh, yes, I can,' Sarah said softly. 'I can't wait forever, Matt.'

Anna had heard and seen enough. She couldn't take any more and headed for the door.

Matt watched her go. 'Where are you off to?'

'Out,' she replied, her tone telling him to mind his own business.

He grasped her arm. 'I'll come with you.'

'Five minutes, Matt. We have to get going,' Sarah reminded him.

'I'll take as long as I damned well like!' he returned over his shoulder.

Webster was crouched on the bottom of the stairs. Anna let him into the sitting-room and closed the door with a feeling of malicious pleasure.

In the garden Matt tried to take her hand but she evaded him and pushed her hands into her jeans pockets.

'I'm sorry about all that,' he said.

'Why are you apologising?' she enquired. 'For your brattish behaviour or the fact that your cousin-stroke-lover turned up here to embarrass you? Don't worry about it. She was here the other day and told me all about your very special relationship.'

He pulled her round to face him. 'Look, don't you start, Anna. We don't have time for all that right now.'

'What a shame. I was going to tell you what she said, about how you really love her, and the mistake you made in marrying me. And how you were forced to stay with me because of Daniel's death, and then there's the possibility that you'd lose your job if we separate. You should have been here, Matt, it really tugged the heart-strings.' Anna laughed bitterly. 'I shouldn't worry too much about her engagement if I were you. I think it's probably a ploy to make you jealous. And it worked too, didn't it?'

His hands gripped her arm tightly, bruising the soft flesh. 'Anna . . .!'

She looked at his face and, though she was deter-mined not to cry, his features were slowly dissolving behind a screen of tears as she felt her anger draining away before the greater pain of knowing she'd finally lost him.

She tore herself from his grasp. 'Just go, now, will you?'

He stayed there, motionless, his hands still reaching for her as she backed away from him.

'Go!' she screamed. 'I never want to see you again!'

And she turned and began to run away from him along the river bank.

CHAPTER EIGHT

AFTER a while Anna stopped and turned back towards the house feeling empty, hollow. Matthew's car had gone and just the small red hatchback stood in the road. In the sitting-room the faint odour of Sarah's perfume lingered, and her used cup sat on the tray.

Also on the tray Anna saw an envelope with her name scrawled on the front in Matt's handwriting. She opened it slowly and withdrew the two small pieces of paper it contained. On one were the words, 'I'll be back as soon as I can!' The second was a cheque for two thousand pounds.

She stared at the cheque. This was the final insult— Matt's parting shot—and she hated him for it.

'Bastard!' she yelled into the silence, and without stopping to think tore the cheque into small pieces and hurled them to the floor.

She paced the room, shaking with rage and hatred. It boiled and seethed inside her, fed by fragments of memory, past hurts and insults jelling together into a single white-hot flare.

There was Sarah, with her cool dismissal of Anna as a person, and Matthew, the selfish, lying bastard who had got having his cake and eating it down to a fine art.

And finally herself, the stupid fool who had let him persuade her into bed with barely a struggle. She could have stopped him with a word. But she hadn't wanted to, had she? Her body had ruled her head as usual. He had touched her and common sense flew right out the window.

He knew her too well, that was the problem. He knew exactly what turned her on. Whatever else had gone wrong with their marriage, sex between them had always been good. And it was so damned humiliating to know he could do this to her, as if she were some kind of sexual robot.

But not any more, she thought grimly. She wasn't going to see him again, not ever. And this time she was making the decisions, not Matt. She'd go and see a solicitor about getting a divorce.

When the rage finally died down she wasn't, as she had expected, swamped by hopeless misery—more a numb, removed feeling, as if she'd done all this before a long time ago.

She'd plumbed the depths once and nothing would ever be quite as bad again. And as she stood there she felt a slight fluttering sensation inside and placed her hands across her stomach.

The baby. She hadn't told Matt about the baby. But so what? She could hardly expect him to be overjoyed at the prospect. He would probably regard it as another complication.

But she'd have to tell him.

She'd come to this decision when she realised someone was tapping on the french window, and looked up to see Doug Whitacker's face peering in at her. Smothering a sigh of irritation, she let him in.

'I thought you had visitors. I heard talking,' he said.

She laughed. 'It was me. I was talking to myself.'

'That's the first sign of madness,' he said predictably.

'Then I must be as crazy as a loon,' she replied. 'Did you want something in particular, or is this just a social call?' She realised as she spoke that she wasn't being very hospitable, but Doug had called at the wrong moment.

He seemed rather taken aback by her direct approach. 'I tried to phone but I think there must be a fault on the line. It's just to let you know that your gran and my mother are staying in town to see a movie this evening. Kate thought you'd worry so I said I'd let you know.'

'Oh ... oh, thanks.' Anna thought she'd better offer him a drink. The used coffee-tray was still on the table and she saw him looking at it.

'Is your husband here?'

'He's gone,' she replied briefly. 'With his girlfriend.'

Doug stared at her. 'Girlfriend?'

'Yes, her name's Sarah Barratt. You've heard of Barratt Oil? She's his cousin, too. They believe in keeping it in the family.

Her voice sounded high and brittle, though she hadn't meant it to. Nor had she meant to cry, but she did, and Doug's arms were round her and she was pressing her face into the masculine roughness of his shabby tweed jacket.

He held her awkwardly, stroking her hair and murmuring soothing things, and, when she'd finished, gave her his neatly folded handkerchief to mop her face.

She smiled weakly. 'I'm sorry, I didn't mean to do that.'

'That's OK, any time. Lucy kind of hinted things might not be going too smoothly between you two, but I didn't think it had gone this far. You should have told us.'

He was hurt because she hadn't confided in them, Anna realised. 'It's not the kind of thing you go round telling people.'

'Anna, we're not people,' he protested. 'If there's anything we can do to help, you only have to mention it, you know.' He flushed and stammered and she was touched.

Impulsively, she took his hands in hers. 'Thanks, Doug.'

Doug shrugged. 'OK?' He gazed at her, his brown eyes reminding her of her grandad's old Labrador dog. 'I'd better be going now, but if you need anything...'

'Thanks, Doug,' Anna said firmly, 'but if I need anything I'll have Gran, won't I?'

'Er—yes, I suppose so. Bye, Anna.'

When he'd gone Anna felt dreadfully alone. Webster eyed her from the corner of the sofa, and when Moses sidled in through the french window the room was filled with the sound of the old cat's soft growls of indignation.

'Shut up, you miserable old thing,' Anna sighed.

Was this how life would be in the future? All the tomorrows stretching ahead until she was old? She couldn't have Matt, so perhaps it was better to stay alone. It was safer that way. You didn't get hurt that way.

Only she wouldn't be alone, would she? In a few months there would be the baby.

In her room the bed was still rumpled; she stripped off the covers and remade it with fresh linen, an act of purification that removed Matt's scent from her bed, but not the agony of loving him from her mind.

'You're what?' Lucy demanded. 'Did you say pregnant, as in baby, bottles, nappies and walking the floor at three in the morning?'

'Yes,' Anna said happily.

'Wow, I like your style, love. Getting pregnant and then ditching your husband. Some people might call that a shade irresponsible, you know.'

'Yes, well, some people wouldn't know the facts, would they?'

'When is it due?'

'The end of March. It'll be a spring baby.'

'Oh, very nice,' Lucy said ironically. 'Does Matt know about it?'

'No, he doesn't.'

'Don't you think it might be a good idea to tell him?'

Anna shrugged. 'He's in Kuwait, isn't he? And I don't have his address.'

'That's no excuse. Write to his office, his mother, anything. You've got to tell him.'

'I know, but I think it might be better to wait until he gets back to England. After all, there's nothing he can do and I don't want him thinking I can't cope without him.'

'Can you cope with this without him?'

Anna thought about that last question as she drove home to the mill. Several weeks had passed and, though she couldn't say life had been particularly jolly, and she missed Matt desperately, so far she hadn't caved in under the strain of being without him. Of course it had helped to have her gran and Lucy around to stop her feeling sorry for herself.

It was autumn, with the smell of woodsmoke, and leaves turning brown, and the brass bowl in the hall filled with purple Michaelmas daisies. Mornings brought mist across the moor, and the harsh cry of rooks in the trees around Crossthwaite Manor, and the twittering of swallows gathering on the telephone wires ready for their migration south.

At the mill she put the car away and went into the house through the kitchen door. Moses rose to meet her, stretching lazily. Webster, asleep on the fridge, ignored her as usual.

She put food down for the cats and began to prepare dinner. She could hear the faint sound of her gran's stereo coming from the pottery, where she was working hard on her Christmas orders.

Anna smiled, thinking of Christmas at Crossthwaite. It was something she and Matt had never experienced together. The Tennant tradition meant the whole family gathered at Ashley with Estelle. Too many people, too much food and drink and false bonhomie, and no one seeming to care what it was all about. Matt had admitted frankly that he hated it, but they had still bowed to the tradition.

Anna shrugged—Christmas was some weeks away, after all. A lot could happen between now and then.

The phone rang. She hurried through to the hall to answer it, hearing with some surprise Estelle Tennant's voice on the other end of the line.

'Is that you, Anna?' she asked carefully.

'Yes, Estelle. How are you?'

'Very well, dear. And you?'

'Fine, thanks.'

There was a pause and Anna could hear Estelle's faint breathing down the line. She could imagine her sitting at her desk, cool and elegant, slender and immaculately dressed, doodling on a jotting-pad with her silver monogrammed pen.

'How are Caroline and Annabel?' Anna asked after Matt's sisters in the hope that it might encourage Estelle to get to the point.

'They're both very well, thank you. Er—Anna, I know you and Matt aren't exactly together at the moment, but I thought I'd better give you a ring rather than have you read about it in the papers...'

Anna's blood ran cold. 'Read about what? Has something happened to Matt?' She tried desperately to ignore the heavy thumping in her chest, the breathless fear that made her legs tremble.

'He's been taken prisoner by the terrorists.'

'What?' The fear was real now, gripping her heart in ice-cold fingers, squeezing, hurting.

'There was a terrorist attack on the oil field. Didn't you see it on the TV news this morning?'

'No, I don't watch TV much.' Anna took a deep breath. 'Tell me about it. What happened?'

'Well, things aren't too clear at the moment. All we can find out is that they took the Barratt Oil people hostage and set fire to some of the buildings. James phoned me from his office in Kuwait this morning. Apparently, the terrorists want freedom for some of their people held in European gaols in exchange for Matt and the others.' Estelle's voice broke on a sob. 'I tried to call you earlier but there was no reply.'

'I was at the shop,' Anna explained, suddenly filled with helpless rage against the cruel, vicious people who deliberately destroyed the innocent in the name of so-called freedom.

And today they had become involved, a statistic: Matthew Tennant, chief geologist for Barratt Oil, leaves a wife... She pressed her hand protectively against the small mound of her stomach... A wife and child.

'What are they going to do?' she asked. 'Is anything being done to help them?' Better not forget there were other men too, other wives and children. She probably knew some of them, those perfectly coiffured company wives, united for once in a common anxiety.

'As I said, things are confused, though we do know Matt and the others were flown out of the area straight away. James seems to think it's a small group of extremists working alone.'

'Thank you for letting me know, Estelle,' said Anna.

'You're still his wife, dear. You have the right to know what's happening. It's best I put you in the picture in case you get reporters on your doorstep asking ques-

tions. After all, we don't want the world to know about
your little marriage problem, do we?'

'How thoughtful.' Let's keep up appearances, Anna
reflected bitterly. Never mind that your only son is in
danger, just be sure no one finds out he's separated from
his wife.

But perhaps she was being a little hard on Estelle. After
all, it must be difficult to forget the habits of a lifetime,
even in moments of crisis.

Relenting a little, she said, 'I think you'd better
know—I'm going to have a baby.'

'Oh . . . how nice,' Estelle replied faintly.

'It is Matthew's child,' Anna added quickly and heard
her mother-in-law's sigh of relief.

'I'm so pleased for you. I'm sure everything will go
well this time and it'll make all the difference, won't it?'

To what? Anna wondered. Did Estelle think that a
baby was all they needed to bridge the gap between them?

'Does he know about it?'

Again that awkward question. 'I'm afraid not,' she
replied.

'Never mind, it'll be a nice surprise for him when he
comes home, won't it? Would you like to come and stay
with me until this wretched business is settled? I'm sure
Matthew would be happier if he knew you were with
me, what with the baby coming and everything.'

Anna imagined herself marooned in Estelle's Gothic
horror of a house with nothing to do all day but wait
for news of Matt and the others, and she shivered.
'Thanks for the invitation, but I'd rather stay here with
my grandmother. Perhaps some other time?'

'As you wish. I'll keep you informed of any new de-
velopments as I get them from James. Goodbye, dear.'

Kate appeared in the doorway and Anna stared at her
with stricken eyes.

'Matt's been taken hostage somewhere in the desert,' she said, and went on to tell her grandmother about Estelle's telephone call. 'Gran, what are we going to do?' she cried.

'We're not going to get into a panic,' Kate said bracingly, her apparent calmness belying the tremble in her voice. 'Matt and the others will be safe. There'll be the usual negotiations and questions in Parliament, but in the end they'll be set free, you wait and see.'

Anna nodded, trying to take comfort from Kate's words, trying not to think about the many people who had been held captive for years. She watched all the news bulletins on TV that day but learned nothing that added to what Estelle had already told her. On the six o'clock edition there was a filmed interview with Sir James Barratt outside his office in Kuwait, where he planned to stay until the hostages were released.

Matt's uncle appeared harassed, his customary cold geniality hidden behind a frown. When the reporter asked if he had any encouraging messages for worried relatives back home, he mouthed the usual platitudes. 'Doing all we can...negotiate the safe release...United Nations intervention...'

All supposed to be comforting, but not a great deal of help to people going out of their minds with worry, Anna thought. She sat on her bed and stared at Matt's photograph as she tried to imagine how he must be feeling at that moment. Was Matt, for the first time in his life, faced with a situation outside his control? Would he feel rage and frustration towards his captors? She was certain he wouldn't make things easy for those who were holding him prisoner.

She wondered if Sarah was in Kuwait with her father. Funny how the thought of Sarah didn't upset her any more. For a long time she had deliberately stopped herself thinking about Sarah, and now it was as though a kind of scar tissue had grown over the pain, numbing, blurring the hard edges, making it difficult to remember how she had felt before.

She looked at her bed, smooth and virginal with its pink sheets and flowered quilt. Unbelievable to imagine it rumpled after sheltering two people making love.

She searched inside herself for some recollection of feeling, some brief memory of what it felt like to be in Matt's arms; his warmth, the feel and scent of his smooth hard skin beneath her hands...

She remembered with her head, but there was no answering response from her body and she was suddenly afraid. It was like trying to recall a dream and finding only misty fragments floating like torn tissue-paper in the wind.

How could she have forgotten something so beautiful? Surely the pain had been better than this empty nothingness?

The hostages soon disappeared from the headlines to be replaced by more immediate calamities. Negotiations with the terrorists had reached a stalemate, though Sir James had protracted meetings with people from the Foreign Office as everyone tried to decide what to do next.

Anna phoned Estelle daily for news, but it was hard to find anything to say once the preliminaries were done with. Conversation tended to dwindle into an uncomfortable silence filled with unasked questions. The calls depressed Anna and made her feel more isolated than ever.

But, despite her constant anxiety for Matt's safety, she was very well physically. She watched for and welcomed the changes in her body with calm anticipation. This baby would be perfect. She felt it and knew.

The time passed quickly. Christmas came and, with it, heavy falls of snow that settled like whipped cream across the country lanes, making travel impossible for several days. The telephone was out of order for a week and, after it was repaired, Anna's first call was from Estelle.

'They're free, Anna,' she sobbed. 'This morning. Isn't it wonderful?'

Anna felt a tightness in her chest and she couldn't speak. She just stood there with the receiver pressed to her ear and listened to Estelle babbling on at the other end of the line. Then she asked, 'Are they all safe?'

'As far as James can make out, they're all fine. He's flying out straight away to make arrangements for getting them home. Oh, Anna, I can hardly believe it after so long... Oh, dear, I'll have to go...' She began to cry and Anna replaced the receiver, suddenly aware that her own cheeks were wet with tears.

How could that be when inside she felt nothing—not relief or joy, nothing? Yet the tears kept on coming, running down her face in a great flood, and she crouched on the stairs, her arms wrapped around her body, and wept until her eyes were so swollen she could barely see through them.

She kept telling herself that Matt was safe, but it didn't seem to register until she saw film on TV of the men being given food at a hotel in Kuwait City.

She didn't recognise him at first; panicking, she searched along the line of men seated at a table answering questions for the Press. Then she saw him, looking pale and strained, different, a stranger behind a heavy growth of black beard. He pushed his hair back from his face in the gesture she knew so well, and she felt herself relax.

He smiled and spoke as someone asked him a question, and Anna knew then that she had expected him to be dead. She had already accepted the possibility of his death, had insulated herself against the pain of it so well that she could feel nothing now she knew he was alive.

Estelle phoned again the next day to tell Anna that Matt wasn't coming back to England with the others.

'There's such a lot of work to be done at the field before they can get into full production again that Matt has to stay and lead the new team James is sending out. It's sensible when you think about it, Anna. After all, he knows the place. He's the logical choice.'

'I see,' Anna replied in a small voice. 'How long will he be staying?'

'It's hard to tell. Things are in such a mess and a lot of the equipment is damaged beyond repair. It may take months, though I expect Matt will come back when the new team have settled in. I'm sure he'll be back before the baby comes, dear. So you see, there's no point you travelling all the way to Heathrow with the other wives to meet the plane...'

'No...I understand. Thank you for letting me know.'

Anna felt a terrible sense of anticlimax as she watched film of the hostages' return to England; the men looked tired and drawn but answered questions with cheerful good humour and looked around as if they couldn't believe the fuss as cameras clicked and whirred, while Sir James beamed like a proud father at a prize-giving.

It was too much for Anna and she sighed despondently.

'Now don't you go getting all upset,' said Kate firmly. 'Matt will be back when he's done his job, and you've that baby to think of, remember!'

The snow melted eventually, and winter relaxed its iron grip on the countryside. Snowdrops appeared in the garden, and the bright yellow stars of winter jasmine.

Anna marked the days off on her calendar, and then, suddenly, it was March and she only had one more week to go, if the baby arrived on time as her doctor seemed to think it would.

'Nothing to worry about, Mrs Tennant,' he said on her last visit to the clinic, breezily addressing her hugely swollen belly. 'Everything's fine.'

Everything would be fine if only Matt was home, she thought gloomily.

It was more than two months since his release and not a word from him, yet he must know she was pregnant by now. Estelle was bound to have told him.

Did it mean he wasn't interested? But surely there must be some reaction, even if it was just to tell her he wasn't interested.

Matthew Tennant parked his Jaguar outside the mill, the feeling of tension which had been growing inside him reaching crisis point as he stopped by the front gate and looked at the peaceful façade.

He knew he should have phoned first, but he had been afraid Anna would refuse to speak to him. He couldn't blame her if she did. After all, it had been more than six months...

Taking a deep breath, he went slowly along the path and round to the back door.

The door was open and the house seemed very quiet, deserted, though in the kitchen the tabby cat, Moses, came to greet him, purring softly.

He had grown into a sleek, handsome animal, confident, self-assured, and Matt wished he could borrow some of the cat's confidence as he walked through the silent house.

There was no one in the sitting-room, and he felt like an intruder as he went upstairs. What could he say if Kate suddenly emerged from behind one of the closed bedroom doors and found him creeping around her house?

He paused in the doorway to Anna's room, hesitated, then pushed it open.

She was asleep on the bed, curled up like a child with her back to him. He could hear her soft breathing and as he walked nearer he saw her face pillowed in her hand, and the soft rosy flush on her cheeks.

Her hair was longer than he remembered, and it lay like a golden halo against the pink flowered pillow. Matt smiled and reached down to touch her shoulder.

Then his hand was stilled abruptly as his glance moved down her body and took in the swollen mound of her pregnancy.

Shock held him motionless; his fingers curled tightly, digging into his palms and his breath stuck somewhere behind his breastbone. Without being aware of what he was doing he backed silently from the room and went downstairs to the kitchen, his mind blank to everything but the numbing fact that Anna was pregnant.

Pregnant!

He had spoken to his mother on the phone this morning and she had said Anna would have a surprise for him when he saw her again. Some surprise! Why the hell hadn't his mother given him some kind of warning?

Why hadn't Anna told him herself? Judging from the size of her the baby was almost due, which meant she must have known about it when he saw her last, in the late summer.

Then the memory of that last time slammed at him with painful clarity, along with almost total recall of all that rubbish he'd spouted about not wanting a child.

Hell, no wonder she'd said nothing. Matt's guts churned with a sick feeling of guilt. If only he had made her listen to him after Daniel died. If only he had made a real attempt to break through the wall of misery she had built around herself, made her see she wasn't alone, that he was hurting too. They might have been able to comfort one another instead of each inhabiting their own private pit of despair. If only he had tried to make her understand that the reason he said he didn't want a child was to insulate himself against the possibility of more pain, not realising... And unwittingly he had rejected her unborn baby.

It occurred to him that he'd thought, Her baby. It was his too, wasn't it?

Wasn't it? Or maybe not. Maybe that was why she hadn't said anything.

He shook his head angrily. 'No, you can't lay that on her. Not Anna, she's different... Isn't she?'

But when had it happened? He could count on one hand the times they'd made love since Daniel was born. The night of the party in New York? Possibly, but...

He clenched his fists, hurting as suspicion chewed at his mind like a hungry rat at the thought of Anna making love with another man, carrying another man's child. There was only one other man in her life—Doug Whitacker. He'd never liked the guy, though he couldn't think of a logical explanation; afer all, he was a decent enough sort, almost too decent if the truth be known. Matt had a deep suspicion of people who appeared without fault. He might have liked Doug a little better if he had shown a spark of human jealousy when Anna had married another man. Maybe he had just been biding his time...

Doug Whitacker...? No, it wasn't possible, was it?

The silence in the house began to get to him and he went back to the kitchen where at least there were the cats to talk to.

Coffee...he'd make some coffee to steady his nerves. He had to get himself together or he'd be a gibbering idiot by the time Anna did wake up...

CHAPTER NINE

THE house was very quiet when Anna woke from her rest that afternoon. She swung her legs off the bed and plodded along the hall to the stairs, glancing automatically through the window overlooking the lane outside as she went past.

There was a black Jaguar XJS by the gate—Matt's car.

Matt's car! She stared at its shiny roof, listening to the helpless thudding of her heart.

Matthew was here!

Realising her hair looked a mess, and her dress was crumpled, she turned to go back into her room, then stopped herself with a soft laugh. Given her present shape, there wasn't much she could do to improve matters. So, with a philosophic shrug, she went slowly down the stairs.

He was standing by the window in the sitting-room, watching the door, watching her.

She paused. His grey eyes were unreadable as they flicked over her. She laid a hand against the swelling mound of her belly in a half-proud, half-protective gesture and his mouth curved in a slight smile.

'Hello, Anna,' he said softly.

Moving on into the room, she replied, 'Hello, Matt. This is a surprise. How are you?'

'I'm fine, thanks.' He indicated an empty cup on the window-sill. 'I hope you don't mind my helping myself. I was longing for a cup of coffee and you were well away up there.'

'Not at all,' she said coolly.

He had been upstairs and looked at her while she was sleeping and she felt uncomfortable with that knowledge. Watching a person sleep was such an intimate thing.

She managed a small smile. He appeared tanned and fit and she wondered if the other captives had recovered as well from their ordeal.

'I was going to ask you how you are, but I can see you're blooming,' he said.

She crossed to a chair, very aware of the huge bulge, her shapeless dress and undisciplined hair.

But at least her hair was clean; she'd washed it that morning before her visit to the clinic, and she suddenly remembered he had always washed her hair for her when she was pregnant before.

Though it was better not to think of before; those kind of memories were like little hammers breaking down the strong wall she'd built to protect her fragile emotions.

'When did you get back?' she asked into the awkward silence.

'Last night. I stayed over at the cottage and drove up here after seeing my lawyer this morning.' He sat down opposite her, looking at her through narrowed eyes.

'You should have phoned,' she said vaguely. 'Gran's gone into town with Mrs Whitacker.'

He smiled. 'Much as I love Kate, I didn't come up here just to see her.'

Anna shrugged, wishing she could think of something clever to say, but her brain felt as if it were wrapped in fog.

He rose to his feet again and walked across the room to lean casually against the fireplace, seeming to tower over her, long and elegant in a dark grey suit, though she noticed he had loosened his tie and the top button of his silk shirt was undone.

'You look well,' she said.

He smiled faintly. 'Surprised?'

'Frankly, yes.' She had expected some signs of strain at least. After all, he'd gone straight back to work after his release, unlike the other men, though as he stood there looking at her, apparently totally at ease, she sensed restless tension in him.

'It wasn't as bad as people back here imagine,' he said. 'We were luckier than the poor bastards who were taken in Beirut. The rebels treated us well, as well as their own people at any rate. There wasn't much by way of home comforts, but we shared what they had. They had nothing against us personally. We'd even worked with some of them at the field. They looked upon us as a valuable bargaining commodity, that's all, and when they realised they weren't getting any backing from other factions they let us go.' He smiled. 'Were you worried?'

'What a stupid question! Of course I was worried.'

He laughed. 'I wonder. Perhaps it would have been more convenient if I hadn't come back.'

She stared at him. 'What do you mean?'

Nodding towards her stomach, he said, 'That, for a start.'

Anna didn't understand, and felt the situation slipping away from her as she saw him looking at her, his eyes cold, like slate. She trembled, clasping her hands tightly together so he wouldn't see.

He smiled nastily. 'Funny you never mentioned it when I was here last. Any particular reason for that...omission, hmm? And don't tell me you forgot. Nobody could be that absent-minded, darling. When is it due, anyway?'

'Next week,' she replied, adding, 'What are you getting at?'

'You should know. Might one ask the name of the proud father-to-be?'

It had never occurred to her he might question her own fidelity. Anger tasted bitter in her mouth, though she remained outwardly calm. 'I suppose you have the right to know the child is yours,' she replied with a shrug.

'What?'

'I said, it's your baby.' So calm in the face of his obvious agitation, she smiled serenely.

'You expect me to believe that?' he persisted. 'How the hell did we manage it—thought-transference? I'll admit I've spent a good few sleepless nights thinking about making it with you, but——'

'It was in New York,' she said, hating herself for explaining what he should already know, but realising she must do it, for her baby.

'That one night?'

'It only takes once,' she pointed out.

'I know, but...come on, Anna...'

She shrugged. 'Believe me or not, I don't care either way.'

'You must care, or you wouldn't be trying to convince me.'

'Think what you like.'

'Do you care?'

Anna's temper snapped. 'Oh, for heaven's sake! Of course I damned well care. This is a baby I'm having, not a litter of puppies!'

'My baby.'

'That's no big deal,' she said wearily.

'You would rather it were someone else's?'

She shrugged again, knowing it would make him angry, then laughed at his anger. 'Does that possibility bruise your precious ego?'

She was goading him. She sensed his uncertainty and inside her a destructive force made her want to hurt him, to take revenge for all her hurt.

He came across the room and crouched down before her, staring into her eyes as the anger between them crackled and throbbed. 'Tell me the truth, Anna, or I'll leave, now, and this time I won't come back!' He gripped her arms painfully. 'Tell me, Anna, for pity's sake!'

He was so near she could see herself reflected in the unfathomable darkness of his pupils. 'What do you want me to say?' she asked. 'I've told you the truth...this is your baby. Whether you believe me or not is up to you.'

With a sigh, he let her go, then gently stroked the marks on her arms where his fingers had bruised the soft flesh. 'I'm sorry, Anna,' he murmured.

She met his eyes; he looked defeated, though there was nothing she could do to help him. His hands moved to touch the mound resting in her lap; they felt warm through her dress, feeling the shape of her. She trembled and tried to pull away, but there was nowhere to go.

'You're bigger than last time,' he said, smiling. He cupped her breasts. 'These too.' Then he touched her face, his fingers caressing her cheek. 'I missed you.' His voice was soft, his eyes vulnerable, yet his touch was firm, decisive, possessive.

Anna was confused. 'Why didn't you come back or get in touch with me?' Her mouth trembled, her voice sounded shrill, accusing, though she hadn't meant it to.

He shook his head. 'I was afraid you didn't want to see me again after the way we parted, but I meant to get back as soon as I could, and then the situation escalated out there.'

His arms slid around her and she sighed, feeling the comfort of him as his mouth touched her neck, her hair, her face, her lips.

'Anna,' he said softly. 'We've been apart long enough. You belong with me and I want you back.'

She pulled from his arms, hardly aware of the tears on her cheeks until his fingers brushed them away. She shook her head and he smiled.

'I only want to hold you. I want to be near you, Anna. Please.'

'Not yet.' It was the same as before; his touch demolishing her defences, his will stronger than her own, his self-assurance defeating her. She couldn't let it happen to her like that, not again.

'Not yet?' he repeated, surprised by her rebuff.

'Matt, I need some time to get myself together. I can't think straight right now.' Please, she implored silently, this is too much for me to take. If you love me, you'll understand.

He stood up, staring down at her. 'You expect me to go? Run along, Matt, there's a good boy, I'm too busy to deal with you right now... Is that it?' He moved away from her, eyes cold, fists clenched.

She sighed wearily. 'You don't understand.'

'Why am I so surprised?' he asked with a bitter laugh. 'I should have had the sense to realise. You have your baby. That's all you ever wanted from me, isn't it?'

Ignoring him she crouched in her chair with her eyes closed, just waiting for him to go and leave her in peace.

She heard the sitting-room door open and close and waited for the bang of the front door. But, instead, Matt went along the hall to the kitchen and after a few minutes Anna heaved herself out of the chair and followed him.

His jacket and tie were hanging on a hook at the back of the door, and, with his shirt sleeves rolled up, he was beating eggs in a bowl.

'What do you think you're doing?' she asked.

'Supper,' he replied cheerfully. 'Omelettes for two. Cheese and tomato OK?'

'Neither, thank you. Cheese gives me heartburn and tomatoes bring me out in red blotches at the moment.'

'So they do...I forgot.' He smiled. 'I'll leave yours plain, then. Are you up to buttering the bread?'

'Why are you doing this?' In spite of herself, Anna did as he asked, and fetching a crusty loaf from the larder began to hack chunks off it with a blunt knife.

Matt removed the knife, substituting a sharp bread-knife. 'I'm hungry. You didn't offer to feed me, so I decided to help myself. Quite like old times, isn't it?'

'It's nothing like old times,' she said sourly.

The eggs ran into the hot pan with a buttery sizzle and she found her mouth watering shamelessly. The omelettes were golden and perfect on warm plates and Anna ate hungrily. It seemed strange to be sitting opposite Matt again and she felt awkward and tongue-tied and wasn't able to meet his eyes.

'I'm glad to see your appetite's improved while I've been away,' he remarked. 'Maybe it's because you're eating for two, as they say.'

'That's a fallacy,' she said, mopping her plate with the last piece of bread.

He laughed. 'Not from where I'm sitting.'

'What was the food like in the desert?' she asked, changing the subject.

He shrugged, 'OK, if you like rice.'

'You don't like rice.'

'You get to like anything if it's all you have to eat,' he told her with a wry smile.

He didn't look as if he'd suffered any privation, she thought, if one ignored the tiny lines around his eyes, and the few odd grey hairs at his temples. 'Would you like a biscuit or some cake?' she asked, relenting.

'Home-made?'

She smiled. 'By my own fair hands, the bread too.'

'And there I was thinking you were helpless without me.'

'I've never been helpless, with or without you, so you needn't think you're doing me any favours by coming back here now.'

He laughed. 'Ouch, I suppose I deserved that.'

'You're damned right, you do! All this time and not even a postcard. You could have been dead for all I knew.'

'I always turn up, like the proverbial bad penny.' He reached across the table to cover her hand. 'I meant to write, but would it have helped, given the way things were between us? There was nothing I could say, apart from I'm sorry, and that had to come in person.'

She eyed him steadily, able to understand, but unable to forgive, just yet.

'How is Sarah?' she asked blandly, and saw him flinch as though she'd touched him on the raw.

'I haven't seen her. Apparently she's busy preparing for a June wedding.' He spoke casually, as if he were remarking on the weather, and Anna allowed none of her inner feelings to show on her face as she said,

'Really? So she's going ahead with her marriage to Andrew Klein after all?'

'Mmm—she doesn't love him, of course, but the thought of the Barratt millions is bound to soften the blow for the poor fish when he realises.'

Anna found it in herself to feel a morsel of pity for Sarah's future husband. Maybe they should get together some time and compare notes...

She smiled. 'Sarah loves you, doesn't she?' Funny how she could actually say it out loud without feeling anything any more.

Matt flushed and glanced away. 'Love means different things to different people.' He sighed heavily. 'I'll admit I was a bloody fool, Anna. You and I were so together that I assumed you'd understand how it was with Sarah and me.'

'What was there to understand?' she asked bitterly. 'I saw enough. Neither of you bothered to hide it from me, did you, though it might have been kinder if you had. Ignorance is bliss, as they say.'

'But there was nothing to hide,' he insisted.

'You think I imagined it all? Those private little jokes, the way she looked at you, the way you looked at her...' Anna stared at him accusingly, her blue eyes wide with remembered pain.

'Listen, however Sarah might have felt about it, marriage between us was never on the cards. I know she had her own ideas but, to put it bluntly, I wasn't about to sacrifice my own happiness for hers.'

'But you didn't mind having an affair with her, did you? A little something on the side,' Anna replied stonily. 'What about that time you went to Munich?'

He shook his head. 'As I tried to tell you at the time, I didn't go to Munich. Things were changed at the last minute and the conference was held in Brussels instead. I only found out myself on the way to the airport. I tried to phone you but there was no reply at the cottage. Then when I got back you started accusing as soon as I walked through the door and never gave me chance to explain.'

Anna stared at him. 'What did you expect, for heaven's sake? Munich, Brussels, wherever, I *knew* you'd been with Sarah. Did you think I'd just accept your infidelity, pretend it didn't matter?'

She rose to her feet and began to pile their dirty dishes into the sink for something to do, anything to get away from the sadness in Matt's eyes.

But he was there behind her, his hands tight on her upper arms as he spun her round to face him. 'You believe I slept with Sarah?' he demanded.

She met his eyes. 'Well, didn't you?' she said softly, realising this was the first time she had actually asked him outright. She shrugged. 'Oh, I'm not saying you were entirely to blame. I was too sensitive and weak. The trouble was, I thought marriage with a man I loved meant happy ever after without having to fight for what I wanted. Then, when reality spoiled my romantic dream, I couldn't cope with it.'

His hands moved against her arms, gentle, caressing. 'Oh, Anna,' he said, 'I have never made love with Sarah.'

She stared at him. 'You expect me to believe that?'

He sighed, then released her and moved away, as though sensing she needed space to consider his words. 'As I said, love means different things to different people. I admit that once upon a time I did feel a kind of love for Sarah, but that was long, long ago, when I was too young to realise what real loving is about. Real loving, Anna... When another person's happiness is more important than your own, and you need to see, to be with, to touch... When the time apart is so much empty space. I never felt that kind of need for Sarah, and she knew it.' He shrugged ruefully. 'My mistake was in assuming you knew it too, but then it's always easy to be wise afterwards, when it's too late.'

Anna looked at him, wanting to believe him as she smiled sadly. 'So, here we are, older, certainly, but wiser?'

'Theoretically, one is supposed to learn from one's mistakes, though in practice I don't think it quite works out that way, do you?' Matt asked wryly.

'Maybe not,' she agreed. It was time to change the subject; there was no point dwelling on things past and what couldn't be undone was best left alone until the pain was less raw.

She began to wash the dishes. 'How long will you be in England?' she asked as Matt took a tea-towel from the rail.

'I'm back for good.' He carefully dried a plate and put it down on the worktop before adding, 'I've handed in my resignation.'

Anna stared at him. 'You mean you're leaving Barratts'?'

He nodded. 'That's right. I've agreed to stay on until they can get a suitable replacement, on the understanding that someone else takes the overseas assignments. Uncle James wasn't too thrilled, but he could see there wasn't a great deal he could do about it.'

'But why? You loved your job.'

He shrugged. 'It's all a matter of priorities. I've had a lot of time to think just lately, and somehow, when I'd added it all up, it seemed as if I was heading nowhere fast, so I figured it was about time to stop and take stock.'

'And?' she prompted gently.

'I've decided to open my own consultancy,' he told her.

'But that's great!' she said. 'Where?'

'I haven't made up my mind yet,' he said, not mentioning that he'd already looked at the lease on an office in the centre of Leeds. It seemed safer right now to give Anna a little breathing-space before asking her to make any kind of commitment.

'I have to drive back to London in the morning to tie up a few loose ends at the office, then I have six weeks' leave. Do you think Kate will put me up?'

'What—here?' Somehow it hadn't occurred to Anna that he'd stay at the mill. Odd, really; after all, where else would he stay?

'Why not? There's the spare room and it's better for me to be here with the baby so near.'

'Your concern is a bit overdue, isn't it?' she said.

He pressed his lips together and she knew he was angered by her apparent rejection. 'You're not leaving me anything, are you?' he said bitterly.

How could he understand that her first instinct was self-preservation? She smiled. 'Don't be angry, Matt. I'd like you to stay, but only if you want to, not because you think you should. So, if you'd prefer to be somewhere else, that's OK by me.'

'You don't need me at all, do you?' he muttered.

'I didn't say that, did I?' She knew he was hurt. Why did she have to feel his pain when he had been so impervious to hers? And what was the use if she was going to have to tiptoe around his feelings like walking on eggshells?

He never used to be so vulnerable—or maybe she hadn't noticed.

She laid her hand on his arm. 'Perhaps it's my turn to apologise... I'm sorry, Matt. I didn't mean to hurt your feelings. It's just that... well, you've always been the strong one, haven't you?'

He'd never shown any emotional weaknesses and she'd always taken his tough self-assurance for granted.

He had led and she had followed; even when they made love she had never taken the initiative from him. She had waited for his kiss, his touch, and felt rejected if he turned from her, when all she'd had to do was reach out her hand and show him, tell him how much she wanted and needed him...

She'd never visualised his pain, his loneliness, yet if he really had loved her...

'Please stay, Matt,' she said softly. 'I think I'm going to need you to hold my hand.'

It was as if a light had been switched on inside him. He raised her hand to his lips, then looked down at the slender fingers, stroking them gently with his thumb. 'It's a deal,' he said softly.

Matt slept in the spare room, and in the morning was up first for a walk along the river bank before bringing Anna a cup of tea in bed.

He helped her sit up, arranging the pillows at her back while she drank her tea.

He smelled of fresh air and aftershave and, dressed casually in a black sweatshirt and jeans, looked clear-eyed and incredibly fit. Anna suspected he was one of those men who would improve with age, like good wine.

'Do you eat breakfast these days?' Matt asked.

'No, but I'll cook yours if you can wait fifteen minutes,' she told him, smiling.

'Can you get near the stove with that?' he asked, grinning down at her bump.

'Near enough to fry your bacon!' she retorted. 'Here, make yourself useful and help me up.' She swung her legs out of bed and he helped her to stand upright with an exaggerated grimace.

'Good lord, is that a baby in there, or a young elephant?' and holding on to her hands he leaned down to kiss her lightly on the lips. 'Did I tell you you're beautiful?'

She moved away, laughing to cover the trembling inside her. 'Why do men always think pregnant women are beautiful?'

Matt shrugged. 'Knowing you've made your woman pregnant is the biggest ego-trip in the world. It proves your manhood, or something like that.'

She looked at him, her face serious. 'Do you really feel like that?'

He slanted a wry glance in her direction. 'You don't want to know how I feel. Shall I run your bath?'

'Yes . . . yes, please.' She turned away, knowing he was looking at her. Her nightdress was thin and he could see her body outlined beneath it. Her hair was tumbled around her face and her eyes were wide and very blue, her mouth vulnerable, trembling. She faced him where he stood smiling from the doorway.

'Lukewarm?'

'What?'

'Your bath?'

'Oh . . . yes, thanks.'

He went and she could hear him whistling above the rushing bath taps as she sat at her dressing-table to pin up her hair. Inside she was panicking. He had her cornered; a smile, a touch, a few words and, though she wasn't exactly putty in his hands, he was crowding her and she couldn't think straight.

And worst of all she was beginning to feel it didn't matter. He was trampling down her carefully erected emotional fences with all the subtlety of a rampaging bull, and inside herself she was helping him.

'Oh, baby, what shall I do?' she whispered desperately.

The taps were turned off and he came back into her room, walking with surefooted confidence, stopping behind her so near that his thighs brushed against her back. She felt his fingers on her neck and jumped nervously.

'You missed one,' he said, tucking a stray curl into a hairpin with the others. 'I like your hair like that, all soft and tumbled. It's very sexy.'

His hands rested on her shoulders, pressing warm through the fabric of her nightdress as he smiled at her in the mirror. 'Come on, Mama, your bath's ready and

I want my breakfast.' And, dropping a kiss on top of her head, he pulled her back against him briefly.

Their eyes met; his warm, laughing, hers bewildered, a little afraid, suspicious. And then he left her alone.

It was easier over breakfast with Kate forming an unconscious buffer between them. They chatted easily; unemotional things, no memories or double meanings.

Matt talked about his experiences in the Middle East, making them laugh with his anecdotes about the men he had worked with, and the things that had happened while they were held prisoner by the rebels.

It seemed odd to be laughing about something so potentially dangerous, but Anna thought perhaps laughter removed some of the fear and horror from his memories of that time.

'What have you been doing for the past few months?' he asked, adding, 'Apart from growing my baby?'

She blushed and went on to tell him about the plans she and Lucy had for expanding the business.

'Is that what you want?' he asked.

'Very much. I think we've gone as far as we can go at our present level, and while we intend to keep Treasures we want to move into textile design, and possibly open another shop in York.'

'Will you be able to fit all this in with having the baby?'

'Of course. I work mainly from home anyway, and I can take the baby with me to the shop, no problem.'

He smiled, though his eyes seemed wary. 'You have it all worked out, then?'

'As far as possible, yes.'

'Well,' said Kate briskly. 'I must get on. I'll leave you two with the dishes, OK?'

'OK, Gran,' Anna replied, wishing she wouldn't leave them alone. But they had to be alone. They had to talk and Kate was sensible enough to realise that even if she wasn't.

She sighed philosophically and looked at Matthew, knowing what was coming next.

'It was no use my sitting on my backside feeling sorry for myself, Matt,' she said.

'No...of course not,' he agreed. 'Do you have enough capital for this new venture?'

'Just about, with a little stretching here and there.'

'You didn't use that cheque I left.' He mentioned it carefully, knowing they were back on sensitive ground.

'No, I didn't. Did you really imagine I would, under the circumstances?'

'It was clumsy of me,' he admitted. 'I only wanted to make sure you had enough to live on while I was away, but realised afterwards my timing was off.'

'It damned well was, and if you'd been here I'd have stuffed that cheque down your throat!'

He cocked an eyebrow. 'One more mistake?'

She laughed. 'What's one more between friends?'

His hands covered hers. 'Friends, Anna? We were much more than friends.'

She looked at his hands, so strong and capable. She had thought her heart would be quite safe in them. 'Let's take it one step at a time, Matt,' she said softly.

'All right, anything you say,' he agreed. He rose to his feet and came to stand over her, his hand gently touching her shoulder. 'One kiss, between friends?'

His fingers cupped her chin, turning her to face him as he leaned down to kiss her. His mouth felt warm and sweet, softly caressing, his tongue-tip flickering across her lips, bringing to life a softness inside which made her pulses throb.

'Some things don't change, Anna,' he murmured. 'The feeling between us is still there. You can't deny it no matter how hard you try. I can see it in your eyes, feel it in your kiss.'

He knelt before her, and his hands moved down to rest on her belly. 'This joins us together for all time.' He laid his cheek against it, then his lips, and they both felt the baby move.

Anna put her hands over his and, seeing his awed expression, smiled. Suddenly it felt so good to have him there with her.

But how long did he intend to stay? It was too soon for her to give him all her trust. She felt as if they were both floating in separate boats on stormy seas; to join him she would have to risk everything, but what if his boat foundered beneath her?

He left for London soon after ten o'clock, promising to be back in time for supper that evening.

Anna remembered then that it was Kate's evening out, and she had invited Doug and Lucy over for supper so that Anna wouldn't be alone.

Matt made a face when she told him. 'Oh, lord, what's-his-name. Can't you put him off?'

'No, I can't. Doug and Lucy are my friends, and it won't hurt you to be nice to Doug for once.'

Grimacing, he laughed. 'All right, if you insist. I'll be on my best behaviour, promise.'

'That'll be the day,' Anna said darkly.

CHAPTER TEN

ANNA felt edgy all that day. She couldn't seem to relax and kept wondering what it would be like to share her life with Matt again. She thought of moving back to London and wondered if she was ready to give that kind of commitment. Right now she couldn't think much beyond the baby. But afterwards Matt would expect her to go home with him.

The problem with that was the fact that she couldn't think of the cottage as home any more.

She prepared the food for supper well in advance, telling herself she was defrosting the fillet steaks because they were quick and easy to cook, and it had nothing to do with knowing it was Matt's favourite food.

Anna fidgeted from room to room, tidying things that didn't need tidying, unable to sit still, unable to think, all her nerve-endings rubbing together until she felt as taut as an overwound spring.

She found herself watching the lane, waiting for the black Jaguar to appear, then laughed at herself for being such a fool; even if he drove like a maniac, he wouldn't be home before seven at the earliest.

Four o'clock, five o'clock, six o'clock. The hours passed with irritating slowness, until at last it was time to go up and change.

She surveyed her assortment of maternity dresses without enthusiasm, finally choosing blue.

'Tonight, I'll be a blue elephant,' she told her reflection. 'Let's face it, there comes a point in every

172

woman's pregnancy when nothing she can do is going to make her look any better, and you, Anna, my girl, have reached that point!'

She brushed her hair, then slid her feet into flat shoes, and had to admit that the finished effect was somewhat less than stupendous.

'Never mind, Matt thinks you're beautiful. You're walking proof of his masculinity.' She giggled weakly and went downstairs.

Kate put her head round the sitting-room door. 'I'm off now, dear. Lucy and Doug will be along in a few minutes so you'll be all right.'

Anna smiled. 'Don't worry, I'll be fine. You go along and enjoy your evening.'

She heard the front door close, and couldn't resist another glance through the window to see if Matt was back. A car pulled up but it was Lucy's tiny Fiat.

Lucy looked elegantly slender in green and entered in a cloud of expensive perfume, then completely spoiled the effect by collapsing on the sofa and kicking off her high-heeled shoes.

'He's not here yet, is he?' she said, sighing. 'I don't know why I love him when he irritates me so.' She grinned. 'How are you?'

'Fine, thanks.' She sat down opposite Lucy. 'Matt arrived back yesterday.'

'He did? Well, what do you know?' Lucy whistled softly. 'So, what did you do, throw him out, or fall on his neck and cry welcome home, all is forgiven? No, come to think of it, if you'd done that he'd still be lying there unconscious, wouldn't he?'

'We talked, and he stayed the night. In the spare room,' Anna added hastily.

'I should think so too.' Lucy glanced round as if she thought Matt might be hiding somewhere. 'Where is he?'

'He had to go back to London, but he said he'll be home in time for supper.'

'So, that's why you're looking all pink and pretty tonight. Is he staying?'

'He has six weeks' leave and says he wants to spend it with me.'

'Better late than never, I suppose. And talking of late, Douglas is again, isn't he? For someone whose life is ordered by the school bell, he's very unpunctual. I find it very annoying in a man. You never know where you are with an unpunctual man.'

Doug arrived twenty minutes late and full of apologies. 'Mother asked me to help her find the cat,' he explained.

'Lord, what an excuse,' Lucy said in disgust.

'She worries if he's out after dark,' Doug replied mildly.

They sat around the dining table to eat. Anna kept looking at the window, watching for the black car, achingly aware of Matt's empty place beside her.

'He's late, isn't he?' said Doug unnecessarily.

'Shut up, Douglas,' said Lucy through her fruit salad.

Anna, determined not to let her disappointment show, laughed brightly. 'He'll have a good excuse, you wait and see.'

'And I'll bet it doesn't have anything to do with finding his mother's cat,' Lucy muttered darkly.

'Shut up, Lucy,' said Doug.

They had an unspoken agreement that their conversation kept off the subject of babies. It was enough for Anna that the bump was there without talking about it all the time.

Tonight they took their coffee into the sitting-room and discussed some ideas for the shop. Anna had resigned herself to the fact that Matt wasn't coming and felt sharp disappointment.

What if he'd had an accident? No, they sent a policeman round to tell people about accidents, didn't they?

'What do you think, Anna?' Lucy asked for the third time.

'Sorry, what did you say?' She shifted her bulk slightly, trying to ease the nagging backache which had come on during supper.

Lucy noticed the movement. 'Are you all right, Anna? You look a bit odd.'

'Just a touch of backache, that's all.'

'Are you sure?' Doug looked at her as if she were an unexploded bomb ticking away across the room.

'I'm fine, stop fussing,' she replied, smiling. 'Now, what were you saying about the shop?'

The conversation went gently to and fro, punctuated by the soft chimes from Kate's grandfather clock in the hall, and Anna ignored the discomfort in her back as far as possible, until it gradually became more insistent, clenching, gripping, and she gasped a little, feeling a sudden knowledge, excitement, fear.

'Doug,' she said matter-of-factly, 'do you think you could run me to the hospital?'

He stared at her, horrified. 'It's not...you're not...you can't—it's not due yet, is it?'

She nodded. 'Next week, but that's near enough.'

'Are you sure? Perhaps if you put your feet up or something?'

She giggled weakly, holding out her hands so he could help her to her feet.

'Don't be so daft, Douglas!' Lucy snapped. She scribbled a note for Kate, then fetched Anna's case and rang the hospital to let them know they were on their way. Doug helped Anna out to his car, and she suddenly remembered the last time—the stately ride in Estelle's Daimler from Ashley Park, where she and Matt had stayed for the last weeks of her pregnancy, with a rug over her knees and Matt beside her, to the small private nursing home Estelle had insisted was so marvellous: 'Caroline had her first there and they're so *civilised* about it all.' Then, it had been the middle of the morning—a wet Thursday morning in January.

She felt another contraction coming. Where was Matt? He should be here to hold her hand. He'd promised.

'Are you OK?' Doug asked tensely.

She smiled. 'Yes, I'm fine, thanks.'

'Of course she's all right. Babies takes hours...I hope,' said Lucy between gritted teeth.

'How would you know, you've never had one?' Doug demanded.

'And whose fault is that?'

The car swerved and Anna clutched her seat. 'Hey, you two, why don't you get married or something and give me a break?'

There was a sudden dense silence.

Matt, you bastard, where the hell are you? Anna cried soundlessly into the dark.

The nurse's rubber-soled shoes squeaked on the polished floor and the sound seemed loud in the hushed silence of the hospital corridor. The lift door slid open with a soft hum and Anna in her wheelchair was pushed inside and turned to face the opening. The nurse smiled encouragingly.

'Soon have you upstairs, Mrs—er——' She noticed that Doug, carrying Anna's case, was hanging back awkwardly. 'Come along, Mr—er—don't dilly-dally. Say goodbye to your mother, dear.'

Anna giggled and said obediently, 'Goodbye, Mother.'

Lucy grinned. 'I'll get you for that, kid. Best of luck, OK?'

The nurse stabbed the lift buttons and Doug turned hunted eyes on Anna.

'Tell her I'm not——'

'Don't worry, Mr—er——' said the nurse, patting his arm.

'Whitacker,' he supplied helpfully. 'And I'm not——'

'Mrs Whitacker will be fine, we'll look after her,' she soothed.

'I'm Mrs Tennant,' said Anna.

'Oh?'

'We're not married,' said Doug.

'Never mind, dear, we don't bother about those little details here, you know. After all, it's the baby that counts, isn't it?'

The lift stopped with a soft sigh and the nurse set off along another corridor pushing Anna in the wheelchair, with Doug trailing faithfully behind.

She directed him to a waiting-room and took Anna's case from his nerveless fingers. 'You just make yourself comfortable, Mr Tennant. I'll send Nurse along to fetch you when it's time.'

'But——'

The nurse was well used to dealing with expectant fathers. 'Don't worry, dear,' she said briskly. 'You just relax and she'll be ready in no time at all.'

Anna felt unreal, detached. The situation was out of her hands. Poor Doug, she thought briefly, before another contraction drove him and everything else from her mind.

Some time later, prepared and relaxed after an injection to ease the pain, she was aware of hushed, urgent voices somewhere near by. Doug was holding her hand, but his grasp felt wrong to her; weak, flaccid, his knuckles cracking when she gripped.

She closed her eyes, giving way to the inexorable driving force within her body, and when she opened them again it was to look into another pair of eyes above a white face-mask, and another hand was holding hers—a large, firm hand, a strong hand that didn't give way when she squeezed.

'Where the hell were you?' she whispered.

Matt pushed the face-mask down impatiently and she thought he said Cowes.

'You told me you were going to London. What were doing in the Isle of Wight?'

'Cows,' he corrected gently. 'Those stupid bovine creatures with a leg in each corner.'

'What about them?'

'I'll tell you later,' he said, smiling.

Anna raised her head off the pillow, looking round for Doug. 'What did you do with Doug?'

'I didn't do anything to the poor devil. He's probably in the men's room throwing up. He's not cut out for this kind of thing, is he?'

'Poor Doug,' she said vaguely. 'He'll never forgive me for this.' She looked up at Matt. He was wearing a white gown over his clothes. 'You look like somebody acting in a soap opera. I thought you weren't coming.'

He pushed the soft tendrils of damp hair back from her forehead. 'I promised I'd be here to hold your hand, didn't I?'

When she woke the sun was streaming across her pillow, and she heard soft voices, laughter and the clink of teacups.

She could remember everything so clearly: the final summit of pain, the soft, warm rush as her baby was born; Matt's arms supporting her so she could see; Matt's voice, hoarse, breaking as he said, 'It's a boy, Anna, another boy!' And she had clung to him, weeping gentle tears of joy and relief.

They had let her hold the baby for a while. They wrapped him in a blue blanket and she had stared down at the small red face, feeling the warm reality of him against her breast, and Matt's strong arms holding them both.

Matt fetched her home to the mill in a taxi, and she stared out at the people, the shops, the countryside, still wrapped in the isolation of the past few days. How odd that everything looked the same when she felt so different. They had stood still while it seemed as if she had flown light years ahead during her short stay in the hospital.

She gazed down at Christopher's sleeping face, his perfect tiny hand gripping a fold in the shawl; her child. She knew him already, her arms and heart were filled with him, as if they were still joined, and she felt complete, whole.

Matt's hand reached across to gently move the shawl away from the baby's face. 'He looks like you,' he said.

She smiled. 'More like my father, I thought, but he definitely has your mouth.'

A silly, musing conversation that carefully ignored the constraint between them. They still had so much to say to one another, yet how to begin?

In the hospital they hadn't had any real chance to talk. Visiting times had been crowded with Kate, Lucy, Doug and Mrs Whitacker. Matt had stayed beside her, smiling, proud, polite, but Anna sensed a feeling of uncertainty in him that made her afraid.

She smiled at him. 'You never did tell me what you were doing in the Isle of Wight.'

'What?'

'The other night. If I remember correctly, you said something about Cowes. Of course, I might have been mistaken. I did have other things on my mind at the time.'

Matt laughed. 'Cows, darling, as in milk and cheese.'

'Don't you ever think of anything else besides food?'

'Occasionally.' He grinned, and the look in his eyes made her heart lurch.

'What about cows?' she persisted.

'I met a herd of them wandering along the road when I was driving back the other night. My car ended up nose first in a wall in the middle of nowhere. That's why I was late. I had to walk five miles to find a phone.'

'You weren't hurt?'

He shook his head. 'It didn't do the car much good, though.'

Anna shivered. 'You always drive too fast,' she said crossly. 'You might have been badly hurt.' Even killed, she added in her mind. Supposing he had never come back...

He smiled. 'Don't look so worried. No harm done, except to the car, and I was getting rid of that anyway. We need something with a little more space in the back now.'

She glanced at him but said nothing.

Kate heard them arrive home and came through from the pottery, wiping her hands, leaning over to look at Christopher's sleeping face with a sigh of pleasure.

'Here you are, Great-Granny, you have him,' said Anna with a laugh. 'I know you're dying to take charge.'

'Heavens, you make me feel a hundred years old,' Kate protested. 'Ah, but he's worth it, aren't you, my little treasure?' And, still crooning, Kate took the baby away upstairs.

Anna sighed happily. 'It's another hour or so before his next feed. Time for a walk round the garden.'

'You're not feeling too tired?' Matt asked anxiously.

'I'm fine, really.'

They walked in silence. The day was soft and warm and filled with the fresh scents of spring. Drifts of yellow and blue crocuses lay across the lawns, among the taller spears of daffodils and narcissi. A froth of pink blossom covered the apple trees in the orchard, and the sun sparkled on the river like diamond splinters.

Anna took a deep breath. 'I love the spring. Everything is so fresh and clean.'

'New beginnings, and all that,' said Matt with a smile.

'I suppose so. You can't imagine anything going wrong on a lovely day like today.'

'I've had an offer for the cottage,' Matt spoke abruptly, not looking at her. 'What do you think? Do you want to sell?'

She stared at him, not knowing what to say, what he wanted her to say. The cottage was part of another life, unreal, like something she'd seen in a film. 'It's...it's up to you.'

He shrugged. 'I wouldn't want to live in it...' He stopped. Had he been going to say he wouldn't want to live in it alone? Anna didn't know, and she couldn't ask.

'Perhaps you'd better sell, then,' she said thoughtfully.

'OK, I'll ring my lawyer and tell him to accept the offer.' They had reached the wall and he stood still a moment, staring out over the river. 'There's the furniture—we'll have to decide what to do about that.'

Hadn't they talked about this once before? Then, she remembered, Matt had been so decisive and she hadn't wanted to listen.

'Let's talk about it another time,' she suggested, feeling suddenly tired.

They went back into the house and Matt insisted she put her feet up while he made tea.

'I called Kate, but I think she's still drooling,' he said, laughing. He sat on the floor and they talked of nothing in particular; just a gentle ebb and flow of conversation, easy, comfortable, carefully avoiding the real issues.

He was leaning against the sofa, inches away from her leg; a long, lithe figure in his black jeans and sweatshirt. Anna lay back on the cushions and looked at him. How long since she had really looked at him, without her vision being clouded by hate or passion or disillusionment?

His profile was still young and firm, and his cleanly cut mouth never displayed a petulant droop. There were laughter lines at the corners of those strange grey eyes, though perhaps the slight frown between his brows was more pronounced than before.

His black hair was longer these days, and she remembered how it used to feel beneath her fingers: springy and clean, and smelling of the spicy shampoo he used.

Her glance moved on downwards, to his neck and shoulders, and his lean, muscular body. She looked at his hands, slender and long-fingered; hands that had touched her, caressed her intimately, given her unbelievable pleasure . . .

She shivered and shifted uncomfortably as memories flickered across her mind like erotic moving pictures, and a hot wave of desire swept through her, surprising her by its intensity.

He felt her move and turned. 'Comfortable?' His eyes held hers for a moment; her face burned and she looked away in confusion. What if he could read her thoughts, if he knew what was going on inside her head, if he read her eyes and guessed . . . ?

'Yes, I'm fine, thanks,' she said.

'More tea?'

She passed her cup, her hands trembling as he took it from her.

'Are you cold? I could fetch a rug.'

'No, it's OK, I'm not cold.' His nearness was setting her on fire. Would he be shocked if he knew what was going on inside her head? Probably. Newly delivered mothers weren't supposed to feel like this, were they?

She tried to concentrate on what Matt was saying. Something about his mother. 'Sorry?' she said.

'Mother phoned this morning,' he repeated. 'She'd like us to go down to Ashley as soon as you feel up to it.'

'Us?' That implied unity, didn't it? Anna thought. 'What did you tell her?'

'I told her we'd let her know.'

Did she want to go to Ashley Park? Anna wondered. Was she ready for that kind of commitment, and all the Tennant relations flocking to view Estelle's latest grandson? Somehow it didn't seem all that important right now when they should be discussing their future.

She eyed him steadily. 'Matt, what are your plans now?' she asked, knowing it was necessary that he tell her.

He shrugged, not looking at her. 'It all depends.'

'On what?'

'On what you want me to do.'

She couldn't see his face, but she knew she hadn't imagined the uncertainty she'd seen before. It was there in the tightness of his jaw, his clenched fists, almost as if he was bracing himself against the pain of her possible rejection, a pain she could feel inside herself.

Anna looked at him sitting there, his head bent, his fingers tracing imaginary circles on the carpet, and love for him welled up inside her, filling her, overflowing from her to fill the room.

And she reached for his hand, knowing that this time it must be she who made the first move.

'I want you to stay with me,' she said. 'I need you.'

He looked at her, his eyes wary, vulnerable.

'I love you, Matt,' she said. 'I love you so very much.'

He knelt, pulling her into his arms, holding her tightly against him, his face buried in her neck as she stroked his hair gently.

'Oh, Anna,' he groaned, 'I love you so much.'

His heartbeats were heavy against her breast, and when he kissed her she tasted the salt of his tears on her lips, and felt his need warming her body, heard his voice saying he loved her over and over again.

And she clung to him, as though without his strength she would melt and float away like smoke and be lost forever.

'Oh, Matt,' she murmured. 'We've been so stupid, wasted so much time.'

'I know.' He looked into her eyes, tracing the shape of her face with his finger. 'I love you, Anna. I never realised just how much until I thought I'd lost you. It really brought it home to me after we were taken by the terrorists.' His mouth twisted in a wry smile. 'Something like that concentrates the mind beautifully, and you realise things you thought important before aren't really worth much of a damn when weighed in the balance against loving and being loved, and knowing you're needed.'

His hand cupped her face and she turned to press her mouth to his palm. 'I need you, Matt.'

There were tears on her cheek and he brushed them away with the back of his hand. 'My pride was hurt when you left me,' he admitted, 'but it made me realise just how much you mean to me.' He held her tightly. 'It was as if somebody had taken all the light and joy out of my life, as if I had nothing. You are my life...'

He drew her into his arms, his voice breaking as he said, 'Oh, Anna, I was so damned lonely without you.'

'I know,' she said softly. 'I know.'

The village was just a few miles from Crossthwaite, and consisted of little more than a dozen houses and a church around a green. Next to the church, the vicarage stood empty, an estate agent's 'For Sale' sign nailed to a tree by the gate.

Matt held Anna's hand as they walked along the stone-flagged path to the front of the house.

'It's beautiful,' she breathed, staring at the weathered grey façade covered with wistaria and Virginia creeper, the mullioned windows, the solid black oak front door.

The large garden was walled in stone to match the house, and there were many mature trees and an orchard, and smooth green lawns and flowerbeds.

'Wait till you see inside,' said Matt. He unlocked the door and stood back to allow her to precede him.

She held her breath as she went inside, seeing a large, well-proportioned hall, with oak panelling and a pale gold stone floor, and deeply embrasured windows through which the sun shone joyously.

Anna stood still, absorbing the atmosphere of the house, the smell of age, of lavender and furniture polish. 'Can we afford it?'

Matt smiled. 'You like it, then?'

'It's wonderful, but can we afford this and your office in Leeds?'

He shrugged. 'With what we got for the cottage, and a mortgage, we can afford it. If it's what you want.'

Anna sighed, visualising them living in this beautiful house, seeing their children grow, growing old together, here, she and Matt.

She reached for his hand, needing to touch him. She always needed to touch him, to have him close, to savour the love they had so nearly lost. Smiling, she said, 'It's what I want.'

He pulled her into his arms and kissed her mouth, and she felt the sudden quickening of his body against her, and the answering quiver of her own flesh.

'Not here,' she gasped, laughing.

'Why not here? Come on, let's have a look upstairs.'

'Is anybody there?' came a voice from the doorway.

They paused at the bottom of the stairs like guilty children as the man from the estate agent came into the hall.

He looked at them. 'Ah, there you are,' he said, and couldn't understand why they both began to laugh.

HARLEQUIN
Romance

A Christmas tradition . . .

Imagine spending Christmas in New Orleans with a blind stranger and his aged guide dog—when you're supposed to be there on your honeymoon!
#3163 Every Kind of Heaven
by Bethany Campbell

Imagine spending Christmas with a man you once "married"—in a mock ceremony at the age of eight!
#3166 The Forgetful Bride
by Debbie Macomber

Available in December 1991, wherever Harlequin books are sold.

RXM

"INDULGE A LITTLE" SWEEPSTAKES

HERE'S HOW THE SWEEPSTAKES WORKS

NO PURCHASE NECESSARY

To enter each drawing, complete the appropriate Official Entry Form or a 3" by 5" index card by hand-printing your name, address and phone number and the trip destination that the entry is being submitted for (i.e., Walt Disney World Vacation Drawing, etc.) and mailing it to: Indulge '91 Subscribers-Only Sweepstakes, P.O. Box 1397, Buffalo, New York 14269-1397.

No responsibility is assumed for lost, late or misdirected mail. Entries must be sent separately with first class postage affixed, and be received by: 9/30/91 for the Walt Disney World Vacation Drawing, 10/31/91 for the Alaskan Cruise Drawing and 11/30/91 for the Hawaiian Vacation Drawing. Sweepstakes is open to residents of the U.S. and Canada, 21 years of age or older as of 11/7/91.

For complete rules, send a self-addressed, stamped (WA residents need not affix return postage) envelope to: Indulge '91 Subscribers-Only Sweepstakes Rules, P.O. Box 4005, Blair, NE 68009.

© 1991 HARLEQUIN ENTERPRISES LTD.   DIR-RL

"INDULGE A LITTLE" SWEEPSTAKES

HERE'S HOW THE SWEEPSTAKES WORKS

NO PURCHASE NECESSARY

To enter each drawing, complete the appropriate Official Entry Form or a 3" by 5" index card by hand-printing your name, address and phone number and the trip destination that the entry is being submitted for (i.e., Walt Disney World Vacation Drawing, etc.) and mailing it to: Indulge '91 Subscribers-Only Sweepstakes, P.O. Box 1397, Buffalo, New York 14269-1397.

No responsibility is assumed for lost, late or misdirected mail. Entries must be sent separately with first class postage affixed, and be received by: 9/30/91 for the Walt Disney World Vacation Drawing, 10/31/91 for the Alaskan Cruise Drawing and 11/30/91 for the Hawaiian Vacation Drawing. Sweepstakes is open to residents of the U.S. and Canada, 21 years of age or older as of 11/7/91.

For complete rules, send a self-addressed, stamped (WA residents need not affix return postage) envelope to: Indulge '91 Subscribers-Only Sweepstakes Rules, P.O. Box 4005, Blair, NE 68009.

© 1991 HARLEQUIN ENTERPRISES LTD.   DIR-RL

INDULGE A LITTLE—WIN A LOT!

Summer of '91 Subscribers-Only Sweepstakes

OFFICIAL ENTRY FORM

This entry must be received by: Nov. 30, 1991
This month's winner will be notified by: Dec. 7, 1991
Trip must be taken between: Jan. 7, 1992—Jan. 7, 1993

YES, I want to win the 3-Island Hawaiian vacation for two. I understand the prize includes round-trip airfare, first-class hotels and pocket money as revealed on the "wallet" scratch-off card.

Name _____

Address_____ Apt. _____

City _____

State/Prov. _____ Zip/Postal Code _____

Daytime phone number _____
(Area Code)

Return entries with invoice in envelope provided. Each book in this shipment has two entry coupons—and the more coupons you enter, the better your chances of winning!

© 1991 HARLEQUIN ENTERPRISES LTD.   3R-CPS

INDULGE A LITTLE—WIN A LOT!

Summer of '91 Subscribers-Only Sweepstakes

OFFICIAL ENTRY FORM

This entry must be received by: Nov. 30, 1991
This month's winner will be notified by: Dec. 7, 1991
Trip must be taken between: Jan. 7, 1992—Jan. 7, 1993

YES, I want to win the 3-Island Hawaiian vacation for two. I understand the prize includes round-trip airfare, first-class hotels and pocket money as revealed on the "wallet" scratch-off card.

Name _____

Address_____ Apt. _____

City _____

State/Prov. _____ Zip/Postal Code _____

Daytime phone number _____
(Area Code)

Return entries with invoice in envelope provided. Each book in this shipment has two entry coupons—and the more coupons you enter, the better your chances of winning!

© 1991 HARLEQUIN ENTERPRISES LTD.   3R-CPS